CLUB TIMES
For Members' Eyes Only

Tyler Murdoch meets Mickey Mouse—fact or fiction?

I'm still in shock over the wedding of Fiona Carson and Clay Martin. Most of us have been wearing black for weeks now that another bachelor is off the market, but survival is our middle name here at Lone Star Country Club. We're sure that Grace Carson gave darling Fiona some cooking lessons, but it's going to take a lawman to keep that filly from wandering all over the stables at night. Not that I'm implying anything by this....

We'd like to wish LSCC-hunk-of-the-month Tyler Murdoch a fabulous journey. When probed over his impending departure, he quirked his handsome brow and said to woman-about-town Maddie Delarue Bridges that he was "going to Disneyland." Say hi to Mickey for us, Tyler. Wait, now that I think about it, do you think he was pulling a fast one on us?

Grace Carson wanted me to drop a little line about our annual "shake-and-cake" dance marathon at the club. You bring a cake, then go out on our ballroom dance floor and shake. We're awarding the winners of the shake-and-cake contest a sumptuous dinner in our Empire room followed by a serenade by our own club manager, Harvey Small (who's been taking Irish Tenor lessons). Don't forget the earplugs!

In good weather or bad, make you best stop of the day right here at the Lone Star Country Club!

About the Author

ALLISON LEIGH

began her career early by writing a Halloween play that her grade-school class performed for her school. Since then, she's delighted to say her tastes have turned from ghosts and goblins to happily-ever-afters. She loves having her characters enter her life for a while, and freely admits that the true highlights of her day as a writer are when she receives word from readers that they laughed, cried, or lost a night of sleep with those characters. Born in Southern California, Allison has meandered her way through several states, finally settling in Arizona with her family, where she maintains a love-hate relationship with the pizza-oven summer heat and the beautiful days that masquerade as winter. She loves to hear from her readers, who can write to her at P.O. Box 40772, Mesa AZ 85274-0772 or Allison@allisonleigh.com.

"I thoroughly enjoyed participating in the LONE STAR COUNTRY CLUB series. Working with the other authors whose work I've so enjoyed as a reader was a particular honor for me. Living for a time with the adventures of Tyler Murdoch and Marisa Rodriguez was a true pleasure. I hope you'll enjoy the ride and feel some of their excitement, passion and love, too."

ALLISON LEIGH

THE MERCENARY

Silhouette Books

Published by Silhouette Books

America's Publisher of Contemporary Romance

Special thanks and acknowledgment are given to Allison Leigh for her contribution to the LONE STAR COUNTRY CLUB series.

 SILHOUETTE BOOKS

ISBN 0-373-61359-8

THE MERCENARY

Welcome to the

LONE STAR
LSCC
COUNTRY
CLUB
EST. 1923

*Where Texas society reigns supreme—
and appearances are everything.*

*A steamy jungle, danger at every turn,
two complete opposites...sparks are bound to fly!*

Tyler Murdoch: He's a vital member of a covert military agency, willing to go where most wouldn't dare. The last thing he needs on this mission is the "help" of a feisty Latina who makes his blood boil and his alpha male libido beg for release. The harder he tries to ignore the smell, the feel of her, the more he knows he'll do anything to make her his....

Marisa Rodriguez: Once burned by love, she refuses to be vulnerable again. But she cannot ignore the passion that smolders between her and the all-too-male mercenary she's been ordered to assist. And as the hot jungles begin to heat up, Marisa knows her resolve is crumbling when it comes to resisting someone she wants so badly.

Missing from Mission Creek: When baby Lena is kidnapped from the Carson ranch, Flynt Carson and the town of Mission Creek embark on a desperate search for the missing infant. The clock is ticking...but they'll stop at nothing to bring the culprit to justice.

THE FAMILIES

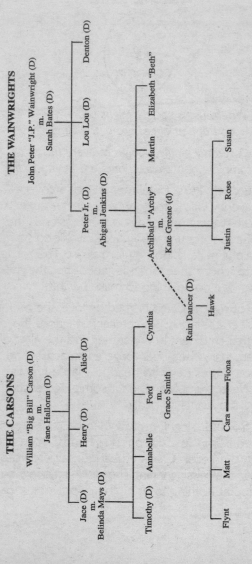

THE CARSONS

William "Big Bill" Carson (D)
m.
Jane Halloran (D)

Jace (D)
m.
Belinda Mays (D)

Henry (D)

Alice (D)

Timothy (D)

Annabelle

Ford
m.
Grace Smith

Cynthia

Flynt

Matt

Cara

Fiona

THE WAINWRIGHTS

John Peter "J.P." Wainwright (D)
m.
Sarah Bates (D)

Peter Jr. (D)
m.
Abigail Jenkins (D)

Lou Lou (D)

Denton (D)

Martin

Elizabeth "Beth"

Archibald "Archy" (D)
m.
Kate Greene (d)

Justin

Rose

Susan

Rain Dancer (D)

Hawk

D   Deceased
d   Divorced
m. Married
. . . .   Affair
———   Twins

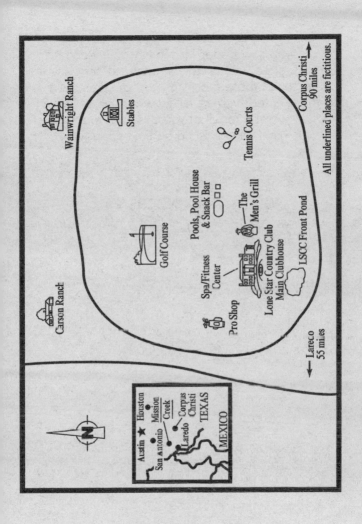

Wainwright Ranch

Stables

Carson Ranch

Golf Course

Pools, Pool House & Snack Bar

Tennis Courts

Spa/Fitness Center

The Men's Grill

Pro Shop

Lone Star Country Club Main Clubhouse

LSCC Front Pond

← Laredo 55 miles

Corpus Christi 90 miles

All underlined places are fictitious.

N

Austin ★ Houston

Mission Creek

San Antonio Corpus Christi

Laredo

TEXAS

MEXICO

This book is dedicated to Judy,
who saw a spot for me when I needed it;
to Ben, gifted with words, wisdom and "knowing it all";
Deb for all those morning walks and great talks; and
the talented women, fellow writers all, of "SSE01."
If it weren't for all of you, this one would never
have been finished on time. Thank you.

One

"Oh, hell, you *can't* be serious."

Tyler Murdoch muttered the words aloud even though there was no one to hear.

He squinted against the sunlight—particularly bright and unrelenting as it reflected against the limitless expanse of arid, tan dirt surrounding the minuscule airfield—and focused on the woman who'd just stepped outside. There was only one small patch of shade afforded by the utilitarian building that served the so-called *aeropuerto* and she'd paused in it. But that didn't mean he couldn't see her just fine.

He wished he couldn't see her just fine. Then he could pretend that she wasn't the person he was there to meet.

Despite the checklist in his hand, he looked her way again. No way could she be the linguistics expert he was to hook up with before flying down to Mezoaya. No damn way.

But he had a bad feeling in his gut that she was.

And Tyler Murdoch trusted his gut instincts. They'd kept him alive too many times in his thirty-five years of life to be disregarded now just because he didn't like the way that woman looked standing over there in that patch of shade. Besides, he'd checked the airfield from east to west and knew that the site was secure. The dust-coated SUV that had arrived and had hastily departed only minutes ago had been exactly the vehicle that Tyler had been watching for. There was no reason for anyone else to be here at this carefully and deliberately abandoned airfield other than the person he was there to meet.

He managed not to swear a blue streak and looked away from her to focus on the clipboard in his hand. But he knew the checklist of supplies by heart and all he saw in his mind was the woman.

No, he didn't like the way the woman looked. The last thing he needed was to be distracted by some female on an op this important. Westin's life depended on Tyler. There was no damn way he'd fail his former commander; he owed the man too much.

None of which alleviated the impatience rising in him, or his annoyance with his superiors for sticking him with that woman. Everyone knew he didn't like working with females. He didn't care what kind of statement that made about him. He wasn't interested in being politically correct, nor was he particularly concerned with equality between the sexes. As far as Tyler was concerned, a woman could sell out her country just as easily as a man.

God knows Sonya had.

He reached through the open door of the plane and tossed the clipboard into the cockpit where it landed next to the captain's seat. His seat.

He might be in charge of this expedition down to Mezcaya, but he was well and truly stuck with Miss Universe over there standing in the shade.

He'd been told his linguistics expert was a native of Mezcaya who'd been in Embassy service for a while, but Tyler was damned if he could see how. From this distance, she looked too young to have done much of anything. Except maybe graduate from college. Maybe.

But then, Sonya hadn't exactly been decrepit with age, either, and she'd managed to cause plenty of damage.

Disgusted with thoughts that were too old to be plaguing him now, Tyler spun on his heel and deliberately strode toward the building. He had a mission to accomplish, and no one, particularly a beautiful woman, was going to get in his way.

It was the heat, Marisa told herself, that made her feel unsteady on her feet. The heat. And maybe a touch of nervousness over the opportunity she'd been presented. It was just so important. If she could only succeed at this, so much could be changed.

The heat and nervousness. Yes, that was all.

She kept her hands folded loosely over the handle

of her slender briefcase by sheer willpower. What she wanted to do was run a hand over her hair; make sure that the unruly waves were still neatly contained in the chignon at her nape. She wanted to shield her eyes from the glare of the sun that even the small overhang above her could not soften.

She watched the dirt cloud up in small puffs around the man's heavy, laced boots as he approached, and told herself firmly that she did not want to turn tail and run. She'd endured things far worse than that steady, grim glare of his. Much worse.

The thought ought to have steadied her. It unsettled her that it didn't. So she schooled her expression and stared right back. Right up until the moment when he stopped, a mere yard away. If it was possible, his hair was even darker than hers. No glints of red, no strands of chestnut, or even silver. It was jet-black. Not quite military short, but definitely an uncompromisingly no-fuss cut. And it suited the blade of his nose, the sharp cheekbones and hard jaw. There was nothing at all about his hard appearance, including the camouflage pants and khaki T-shirt that strained against his broad shoulders to suggest he was anything but what he was—a warrior.

Pressing her lips softly together, she inhaled deeply and kept her leather-shod feet firmly planted. She'd been warned that Tyler Murdoch might be somewhat difficult to work with—his expression certainly indicated just that—but she was on this mission whether he liked it or not.

She stuck out her hand in greeting. "Mr. Murdoch."

His eyes, as darkly brown as the coffee her *abuela* had fixed every morning of her childhood, flickered disinterestedly over her outstretched hand. "They didn't tell me that M. Rodriguez was a woman."

As a beginning, it could have been worse. It also could have been better. "Marisa," she supplied, aware of the difference between his softly drawling speech—pure U.S. of A—and her speech that still held a trace of her homeland no matter how many diction classes Gerald had foisted upon her.

She finally lowered her hand and took a slender envelope from the pocket of her briefcase. She held it out. "A letter from the former ambassador to Mezcaya."

He took the envelope from her, sliding it in his back pocket without a second look. "Do you have any other ID?"

"Um, well, yes." She unzipped another pocket and pulled out her wallet, flipping it open. She thought he'd just look at her license, but he took the wallet right out of her hands and began removing cards, not even studying them first.

"What are you doing?"

He handed her back the wallet, sans license, in-

surance cards and anything else that personally iden-
tified her. "My job," he said flatly and moved past
her through the door.

She shifted, hurriedly following him into the shadowed interior. "Don't you want to verify my credentials? You didn't even read the letter from Ambassador Torres."

He slowly turned his head, looking at her over his
shoulder. And Marisa couldn't prevent the tremors
that skidded down her spine. "If you weren't
M. Rodriguez, you'd hardly be here at this miserable
excuse for an airfield. What happened to the driver
who brought you?"

"He headed back to the city." A fact she felt sure
the man already knew. Since the moment she'd accepted the invitation to participate in this "expedition," her life had become a whirlwind.

Tyler had gone into the minute office in the rear
of the building. "Didn't it bother you to be left here,
alone?" he asked. "This place is a long way from
civilization."

She couldn't see what he was doing in the office.
She raised her voice a little. "I wasn't alone. *You*
were here." She simply would not admit to any unease even though it was greater now than it had been
when the driver tore off in a flurry of dust. Tyler
would undoubtedly take her unease as weakness, and
she'd learned long ago to keep displays of weakness

to a minimum, particularly when dealing with tall, formidable-looking men.

Another leftover from Gerald.

Tyler came back out of the office. He barely spared her a glance as he headed for the door. "What makes you think I'm safe?"

Her lips parted and she blinked. The driver had assured her that the man standing by the sleek plane was indeed the one she was to meet.

He was just trying to frighten her.

She headed after him. Her briefcase bumped her knees so she slid the long strap over her shoulder. "Mr. Murdoch—"

"We're wheels up in five," he interrupted flatly. "If you're gonna back out, do it now. We've got several hours of flight time ahead of us. If this place seems rough, it's only going to get worse."

Her chin lifted. "You forget, Mr. Murdoch, I come from Mezcaya. I grew up in worse." And she had dreamed for years of leaving it.

His lips twisted, making his hard features look even harder. "I don't forget anything, honey."

The words seemed like a challenge, and anger sparked inside her. But she couldn't afford to lose her temper over this man's arrogance. "Nor do I, Mr. Murdoch," she assured.

Tyler looked down at her, noting the perfectly oval face and the delicate golden-toned skin strikingly offset by her drawn-back hair. Even in the dimness inside the building, it held the gleam of onyx and for a second she reminded him of someone, though he couldn't quite place whom.

He'd freely admit she was an honest-to-God beauty, but it was the glint in those almond-shaped golden eyes that piqued a reluctant interest deep inside him. He reined it in. He was on duty. She was a woman and he was stuck with her. "Four minutes." He walked through the doorway.

"My suitcase is by the corner of the building," she said after him.

"Then I guess you'd better get it," he suggested blandly, and headed toward his plane. He almost smiled as he heard the soft word she muttered behind his back. He'd been called far worse.

He'd flown to this bit of nothing in Guatemala and had been on the ground less than two hours. Still, Tyler did a quick walk around the plane. He climbed up and took a last look in the fuel tanks because every pilot worth his wings knew that fuel gauges were notoriously inaccurate, even in as sweet a honey as his Pilatus. When he was satisfied that all was as it should be, he looked beyond the wings of the plane and wondered how a runway could be so damn bad and still be called a runway.

He climbed inside the plane and watched Marisa haul her suitcase over the hard-packed ground toward the plane. She had to lean back against the weight of it, and he could only imagine what she'd packed. Hair stuff. Makeup. Every single useless thing imaginable, he figured, considering the place they were headed.

She was still grumbling under her breath when she hefted the case through the passenger door and climbed in after it. Tyler wasn't so language-challenged not to know that she was seriously besmirching his ancestry in Spanish. Frankly, as far as he was concerned, she was pretty much on target.

Amused despite himself, he looked back through the opened cockpit door to watch her settle in one of the four passenger seats. Behind the seats, the rest of the cabin was used for cargo, of which Tyler had plenty. For anyone curious enough to look, Tyler would appear to be an American very anxious to get lost in another country.

Marisa was wiggling in the spacious leather seat, and her cheeks turned pink when she realized he was watching her. "It's a nicer plane than I'd expected," she admitted.

"My plane isn't run-of-the-mill enough for the casual drug-runner?" It was spacious, but he still had to bend over to move around as he secured the passenger door. He'd already checked the cargo door.

"Is that what we're supposed to be? Drug runners?" Her eyes had gone wide, making her look every bit as young as the twenty-five her license had divulged.

"The only thing we're *supposed* to be is inconspicuous," he said as he belted himself back into his seat and cranked up the engine.

"And being dismissed as a drug-runner is safer than being suspected of something else," she concluded, raising her voice to be heard above the engine.

"It's Mezcaya." What else was there to say? The particularly turbulent little Central American country was torn between a terrorist group known as El Jefe, and the rebellious natives who neither honored El Jefe's rule nor the ineffectual leaders who governed the land. It would be better to be mistaken for drug-runners than what they really were.

Which was one of the reasons he was using his private plane. Made it even more removed from military operations.

Marisa swallowed the unease that ran through her as Tyler donned a pair of headphones and set the plane rolling slowly across the rutted runway.

Mezcaya. Her homeland. Would it even welcome her back?

Don't think about that.

The plane was gathering speed, admirably skimming over the ruts, but still it was rough going. She leaned over and slid her briefcase more firmly under the seat, then sat back and closed her eyes. She'd never been terribly fond of flying but had learned to tolerate it, first for her duties with the Embassy, then later because of Gerald.

Still, this plane, as nice as it was, was considerably smaller than the jets she was accustomed to, and her fingers curled anxiously around the armrests when the nose lifted from the ground and the sharp ascent pressed her back into her seat.

There were a dozen questions she wanted to ask Tyler Murdoch. But through the narrow cockpit opening she could see that he still wore his headphones, and even if not for them, she knew he wouldn't welcome any questions or comments from her.

His attitude couldn't be clearer. He didn't want her to accompany him to Mezcaya. The only thing she wasn't sure of was whether he'd heard about her, and his lack of welcome was because of that, or whether he had other reasons.

She knew he was part of some special unit with the military. The former ambassador had told her that, along with a few other, scarce details. Though unlikely, she supposed it wasn't out of the realm of possibility that he might have met Gerald and heard the rumors surrounding her.

It had been four years, yet even now, Marisa had to consciously release her anger over Gerald's lies. He'd claimed to love her. But he'd ruined her. Left her career in tatters. And her family—

Don't think about that.

It was a much too frequent mantra.

The plane leveled off, and Marisa's ears stopped popping. She reached for her briefcase and drew out a file. Among other things since she'd "left" embassy service, she'd found work as a freelance translator for a few small-press publishers. The latest project was a paper on the long-term effects of video game usage by myopic users. She was translating it from English to Italian.

A few hours later, she'd made little progress on the dry project, because her eyes kept straying to the oval windows on the other side of the empty seat beside her. She sighed and put the file back in her briefcase, unclipped her safety belt and slid into the window seat to look out.

The landscape below was lush, green...and surprisingly close. Startled, she jerked back and stared at the cockpit. Surely they weren't supposed to be flying so close to the ground. The treetops looked so close that it was a wonder they weren't hitting the wings!

All the nervousness that she'd ever felt about flying climbed into her throat, leaving one choking knot. She slid out of the seat and hurriedly made her way forward to duck into the cockpit.

Tyler knew she was there before she could say a word. He pulled off the headset that held little more than static. "Head's behind that door there."

She blinked. "What? Oh. No, no, I don't—I—"

Her lips firmed and she leaned closer. "What are you doing flying so low? Surely that's dangerous."

"Everything's been dangerous since takeoff." He didn't want her up here in the cockpit. It was close enough without adding her shapely self to the mix. If he moved his arm two inches, he'd be brushing against the curves contained within that scoop-necked jacket. It buttoned all the way up the front, but still exposed the hollow at her throat, the golden creamy neck—

His head filled with curses that some forgotten sense of decency kept him from mouthing. "Either sit down here, or go back to your seat and buckle in." He sounded like a grouchy old man, and he didn't much care. Better that than a red-blooded male way too aware of a female he didn't want around, anyway.

She confounded him by taking the seat beside him. And he couldn't help but appreciate the view when she arched her back a little, reaching for, then fastening, the safety harness. Her knuckles were nearly white as she clenched them together in her lap.

"Don't touch anything."

Her nose went up in the air. "I wouldn't dream of it."

His jaw ached. He focused on the view beyond the nose of the plane.

He was flying low for a reason, but he had no

intention of explaining himself. And when they got Westin to safety, he was going to have a talk with TPTB of Alpha Force. Apparently they didn't take his no-women rule quite seriously enough.

He tuned out his companion and her white knuckles, and focused on the heavy forest below. This corner of Mezcaya near the border of Belize was mostly uninhabited. He wanted to make sure he didn't show up on any radar and he wanted another look at the terrain while he had the chance. His last foray into Mezcaya had been too brief to suit him.

He'd studied the maps, of course, well enough to memorize them. But maps were one thing; seeing the land for himself was another. Soon enough, they'd exchange the plane at a designated place just across the border in Belize for a less conspicuous mode of transportation, and he wanted every advantage he could get before then.

Her knuckles were still white.

He stifled a sigh. "You were born in Mezcaya?"

She didn't look at him. "Yes."

And she'd been in Embassy service. Probably the pampered daughter of some dignitary. No wonder she looked like Miss Universe. "How many languages do you speak?"

"Thirteen."

Definitely one of the privileged few from Mezcaya. The average family didn't school their sons, much less their daughters, beyond primary. "Impressive."

Her head slowly turned toward him, her golden eyes skeptical. "Why do I doubt you mean that?"

"I don't say what I don't mean."

Her expression didn't change. "Perhaps we'd be better served by discussing the task ahead of us."

"Task." The word felt as insubstantial on his tongue as it did to describe the operation. "Weren't you briefed?" If she hadn't been told too many details, he'd come up with a way to keep her from accompanying him all the way to the compound.

"I know we're to try to rescue an American officer named Phillip Westin."

"I *will* get him back." Tyler corrected flatly. "There's no 'try' about it."

"El Jefe has him."

"That won't stop me."

"Us."

His jaw ached even more.

"Others have failed," she persisted.

"I—*we* won't."

"How do you know that?"

"Because we're not going in the way they'll expect." His friend Luke Callaghan had already been injured and was even now recuperating at a hospital in Texas. Tyler still had a hard time believing his old friend wasn't just the millionaire playboy they'd all believed him to be. And if it weren't for the fact that Luke had been blinded during his battle to save Westin, Tyler would probably still be pissed about the revelation that Luke was an operative with a co-vert civilian agency, involved in tasks eerily similar to those in which the Alpha Force engaged. But Luke's methods had still been of the traditional bent.

"You mean, we're going in as domestics."

He slid the plane in a slow bank, then dipped into the valley between two mountains. A river snaked below them, glittering like a strand of diamonds. They were no longer skimming the treetops. It was so damn beautiful it was hard to believe anything bad ever happened in this country. "Yeah." He glanced her way. "We'll have to go in as a married couple."

That seemed to startle her. "Why?"

"Because you're a woman."

"And you're none too pleased about that."

"If M. Rodriguez had been a man, we could have posed as brothers."

"Even though one wouldn't be able to speak Mezcayan, much less Spanish." Her voice dripped disbelief.

His inability to fully master foreign languages was something Tyler had long ago accepted. People had different gifts. His was more along the lines of blowing things up than conjugating verbs. Which didn't mean that hearing her observation did not rub him wrong. "I don't need to do much speaking," he said flatly. "That's what they gave me *you* for."

"Then I'll be your sister instead of your brother," she said reasonably.

"You'll be my wife."

His words seemed to float around the cockpit, blurring into the sound of the wind outside the plane, the steady drone of the engine.

He saw the way her shoulders stiffened, as if the statement was as abhorrent to her as it was to him. "What if I don't agree to that?"

"Then I'll leave your butt in Belize when we land in a few hours."

"And you'll never make it from there across Mezcaya and into El Jefe's compound without me."

"Don't be so sure about that." He would make his way to *Fortaleza de la Fortuna* whether she accompanied him or not. He would infiltrate the infamous compound, locate the damned cave that Luke had spoken of, free Westin and get the hell out of there, even if he had to blow up the entire compound and everyone in it in the process.

As far as he was concerned, destroying El Jefe's compound was just fine with him. The world would be a better place without the terrorist group. Only he'd been ordered not to incite an international incident. Which meant he had to use some finesse, exercise some restraint and get it done in the time he'd been allowed before the Brits took over and did God knew what.

"El Jefe runs that entire region of Mezcaya."

"Tell me something I don't know." That was one of the reasons they were flying into the opposite side of the country.

She rattled off a stream of incomprehensible words. Mezcayan, he assumed. "Your point?"

She smiled faintly, looking superior enough that he wanted to hand her a parachute and show her the door. "I said that you'll never make it through the gate of *la Fortuna,* unless you can speak Mezcayan or are very closely tied to one who does. That's how El Jefe ensures some modicum of loyalty from those who live there.

"El Jefe may be scourge to the rest of the world, but to a great many citizens of this country, it is their savior. It feeds and clothes them. Provides for their children. Its compound isn't merely a well-secured estate, Mr. Murdoch, it is virtually a state of its own. The language isn't taught in schools. The government has decreed Spanish to be the official language, quite possibly as a direct statement against El Jefe. There are some that believe the language has been kept alive for the past few generations strictly because of El Jefe's influence. Mezcayan is handed down from parent to child and so on, and only those who are natives of the land are likely to speak it well. Which means that you need *me* to get you through the door.''

Everything she said was true. But she'd left out one detail. And much as he didn't want her there with him, he wouldn't be responsible for harm coming to her, something his damned superiors had to have known. But as much as Tyler hated feeling manipulated, he was more concerned with his obligation to Westin. "We won't go through unless you have the protection of being a married woman."

He saw unease ripple through her eyes. Her lips parted, then closed.

"You know what I'm talking about."

She looked away. "There have been rumors."

"Unless you're a nun or married—which El Jefe seems to have an unusual respect for considering everything else—women are fair game. Willing or not, El Jefe doesn't care. If you've been raised in the compound, you'd possibly be taken as a wife or mistress by one of the officers should one take a shine to you. Gain their disfavor and you'd be sold off to the highest bidder. Or worse."

"Rumors."

"You want to take a chance that they're not just rumors? Come on, M., look in a mirror. They'll be lining up like hungry coyotes to see who gets the first taste. First tastes probably go to senior officers. The generals of El Jefe. Remember that British reporter a few years ago? She managed to infiltrate the compound, even managed to keep her cover intact. But she was—''

''Stop.'' Marisa didn't need him to go any further. He could have no idea how close his words struck. No idea, whatsoever.

It was just that he, like so many others in the free world, had probably seen the news story. It had been splashed across every paper for days. The woman, barely a reporter at all, had been raped then abandoned outside of the compound. When she was found, she was taken to a hospital in Mexico where her story came out.

What the news stories hadn't said, however, was what happened *after* the hospital. The woman eventually committed suicide, unable to withstand the effects of her encounters with El Jefe. She'd left behind a child and a lover beset with grief.

The knot in Marisa's throat had extended down to her stomach. She couldn't let fear stop her from following through on this. There were too many reasons why she needed to succeed. ''So, I'll be a nun.''

''Nobody with two eyes in their head would believe that.''

She bristled. ''Why not? Is there something…heathen about me, Mr. Murdoch?''

His gaze roved over her, making her feel hot and cold all at once. She didn't like it. She didn't like him. Knowing that this arrogant stranger could have any kind of effect on her was simply unacceptable. And being told in that unrelenting manner that she would portray his wife was just too close to orders that Gerald had once decreed. "I could act the nun well enough. For a little while, at least. I was raised as a Catholic and—"

"No."

"Why not?"

"Because I couldn't pass as a priest, and there would be no other reason for me to be accompanying you."

"Of course you could pretend to be a priest. For a little while. We could say…well, that your vocal cords were injured so you can't speak, or something."

"Unless my eyes were bandaged they'd still see the way I look at you."

Marisa flushed.

"Besides," he went on, as if regretting his admission, "there's no reason why a strange priest and nun would gain access to *la Fortuna*. But they're constantly taking in servants. It's the only way."

Silence hung between them for an endless moment. Then he spoke again. "Come on, Marisa." Tyler's voice was low, gentle. And she immediately distrusted it. "There's nothing important enough for you to want to do this."

Distrust, indeed. Her voice cooled. "My reasons *are* important, Mr. Murdoch, so please don't make the mistake of dismissing them. Why is it so important to you to find this man?''

"Because I owe him. I was a hostage once and if not for Lieutenant Colonel Phillip Westin, who lived, ate and breathed for his men and didn't give up on us, my friends and I would all be dead by now. I'm prepared to lay my life down for that man.''

Whatever Marisa had expected, it wasn't that. However, Tyler wasn't finished.

"But I'd just as soon get out with us still alive,'' he added. "Which means that you don't make one move without my say-so. I don't care how well developed your Mezcayan heritage is, or what your reasons are for horning in on this op. There're two people in Mezcaya that I trust, and one of them has been held captive for months now. So do what I say, when I say, and maybe, just maybe, we'll come out of this with our skin intact.''

"And the other person you trust?'' She wasn't sure she wanted to hear the answer.

Tyler was no longer looking at her, but out the window beside him. "Isn't you.''

Two

Well. That was clear enough.

Tyler didn't trust her. She didn't particularly trust him, either, so she supposed that made them even.

"You've got different clothes?"

The absolute and utter change of topic surprised her. She looked down at her linen pantsuit. It had been excruciatingly expensive, but necessary, if she was going to make it back to the life she'd once had. She couldn't show up as a representative of former Ambassador Torres in the polyester uniform she wore at the restaurant.

He'd made no sound whatsoever, but she could sense his impatience. "Yes, of course I have different clothes with me," she answered.

"So you'll look like a local? A likely candidate for a servant?"

"Yes."

"Thank God for that," he muttered.

Oh, she really didn't like this man. "You don't exactly look the part of a servant, either," she retorted. What he did look like was a one-man military unit who'd never taken orders from anyone in his life.

If he took exception to her tone, she didn't know it. "We'll both change when we land," was all he said.

She realized her teeth were worrying the inside of her lip and made herself stop. She didn't want to pretend to be anything with this man, but if she had to, she'd do what was necessary.

"When will that be?"

"Soon enough."

Her lips tightened. "Mr. Murdoch, things might run more smoothly if you'd just tell me what your plans are."

"I'll tell you what you need to know when you need to know it."

She blew out a noisy breath, then unsnapped her harness.

"Where are you going?"

"To sit back there with the cargo. It's friendlier than you are." Her annoyance was a bristling, physical thing as she brushed past him through the cockpit door.

The bare skin of his arm tingled from the contact. He looked back at her. He was acting like an ass. He knew it. She knew it. She was beautiful, sexy as hell with her hair tied back in that tight knot, and he didn't want to need her help. He didn't trust her but he had to work with her.

Damn El Jefe!

He ran a practiced eye over the instrument panel, then looked back at her.

She was just fastening her seat belt, her head lowered as she fumbled with what should have been an easy task. A long strand of hair had worked free of her knot and clung to her cheek. She dashed it away with an angry motion, her gaze meeting his.

She looked away, but not quickly enough.

He thought he was immune to crocodile tears. Sonya had been able to summon them at the drop of a hat.

Hell. A conscience was mighty inconvenient, sometimes. "Do you have brothers and sisters?"

"Why?" She was suspicious.

"Only making conversation." He turned back around, automatically checking his panel.

After a long moment, she answered. "I have a sixteen-year-old sister and…"

He glanced back at her when she paused.

"Three brothers," she finished flatly. But at least her tears were nowhere in sight. Then her eyebrows rose and with extreme politeness, she said, "And you?"

"I'm one of a kind." Though, really, he had no way of knowing whether the man who'd fathered him had sired a dozen other offspring, since Tyler never even knew the guy.

"Indeed." Her tone was dry. "What a pity the world doesn't have more *just* like—" She gasped when the plane shuddered and suddenly lost altitude.

He snapped around just in time to see a piece of cowling fly from the nose. Fury followed hard on the heels of disbelief at the sight of his plane damaged. Wounded.

Under his hands, the stick jittered. His adrenaline shot through the roof as he struggled to maintain his heading. "Come on, baby," he whispered. "Keep it together for me." He raised his voice. "Get up here," he ordered.

Marisa was already slipping into the right seat, fastening the harness. "Take those binoculars, there," he ordered.

She immediately reached for the leather case. "What am I looking for?"

"Anything," he said flatly. It took some doing, and the execution was hardly textbook, but he turned the plane, changed headings. Coaxed some precious altitude from the reluctant controls. Keeping one eye on the instruments, he looked out the window. "He's probably got a truck. A Jeep, maybe."

"He?"

"Whoever shot at us."

"Shot!" She swallowed audibly. Holding the

small, powerful lenses to her eyes, she peered out the side window. "*Dios.* All I see are trees!"

At least she wasn't screaming in hysterics.

She *wasn't* screaming in hysterics.

Tyler grabbed her arm and yanked her around. The binoculars tumbled out of her hand and bounced with a clank off the instrument panel to fall on the floor near her feet.

She stared at him like he was mad. "What is wrong with you?"

"Who'd you talk to?"

"What?"

"Come on, princess, spill."

Realization dawned. Marisa's fingers curled against her palms, wishing that they were clawing out his eyes, and the strength of that desire horrified her to her soul. "You think I had something to do with this?" She yanked against his grip, but he merely tightened his fingers. "Let me go!"

"Tell me, Marisa. You know so much about *la Fortuna.* Maybe you're already one of the El Jefe whores. They'd consider you expendable to keep me from getting to Westin."

She saw red. Literally saw a haze of it come over her vision. Gerald had called her a whore. He'd been wrong, too. "You are vile," she snapped, and yanked again at her arm. She succeeded in breaking from his hold only because he suddenly turned back and had both hands on the stick as he crooned—there was no other word for it but crooned—to the plane.

It chugged, it jerked, it shuddered.

Then all was silent.

The wicked-looking prop slowed until it turned lackadaisically, like some exotic wind decoration.

Her heartbeat sounded loud in her ears.

She could hear Tyler's breath.

She stared at the prop, wishing with everything inside her that it would turn, whip into the revolutions that were so fast, they seemed invisible. Wishing she was once again near deafened by the hum of the engine that could be felt all around them.

But nothing.

She swallowed, not daring to look at Tyler, because if she did, this would all seem too real, too desperate.

Then she realized it wasn't really all that silent, after all. And she did look across at Tyler.

The ominous sound of wind rushing outside the plane grew to a roar as the plane bulleted through the sky with no power and only a grim-faced Tyler at the controls.

She stared again out the nose of the plane, seeing the damage, feeling dizzy. "We're going to crash," she said faintly. All she'd wanted was to undo the damage that had been set into motion by her leaving Mezcaya. Was this, then, to be her final punishment?

"We're not going to crash," Tyler gritted beside her, as if by willpower alone he could prevent that from happening.

She looked at him, saw the tendons in his arms stand out as he struggled with the controls, the sheen of sweat on his face. "I didn't do this to us," she whispered.

"You better hope to hell I don't find out differently, or I'll finish off the job that shooter didn't."

She believed him.

Tyler didn't have time to worry about Marisa's pale face or the way she was staring out the window. There was no mistaking the abject terror in her face, whether she knew about the attack beforehand, or not.

He needed a place to land and he needed it yesterday. Had El Jefe somehow tracked them? Or was this an act by one of the natives, the ones who were determined to protect their way of life even if that meant shooting at a suspicious plane circling over their territory?

They were losing altitude. He'd been heading back toward the river, and he could just spot it in the distance. If he could just coax a few more...

"Brace yourself," he ordered.

And then they were tearing through the trees,

heavy branches crashing against them, toppling over beneath them. He barely had time to cover his own face with his arms after they cleared the rest of the trees and headed straight into the river.

Marisa screamed.

Water splashed up and over the nose of the plane.

Eerie moans filled the air and metal screamed as its momentum was abruptly stopped.

Marisa and Tyler, strapped in their safety harnesses, bounced around like rag dolls in the grip of a rambunctious, cartwheeling child.

Cargo broke free, tumbling, bouncing, breaking.

Then all motion ceased, jerked to a cruel, bone-bruising stop as the plane settled, tilting crazily against some immovable force.

Dazed, Tyler gingerly shook his head. He realized water was lapping higher and higher against the side of the plane. He ripped off his harness and leaned toward Marisa, gently tipping back her limp head. She'd struck something when they'd hit. Her forehead was bleeding. But she was breathing. And when he said her name, her mouth moved in reply.

Then her eyes opened slowly and stared, glassy, at him. "You're bleeding," she murmured.

Later, he might wonder over the relief he felt. But for now he didn't have time. "So are you," he said, and pushed himself painfully out of the cockpit. "We've gotta get out of here before the plane floods.'' He kicked her briefcase out of the way as he made his way to the passenger door. It was buckled, and no amount of muscle would get it open.

He headed through the mess of supplies for the cargo door toward the rear of the plane. That opened, but it also let in a wave of cold water. He swore. ''Marisa!''

Marisa had stumbled out of the cockpit behind him. ''Tell me what to do.'' She still looked unsteady.

''Get that duffel there. The black one. Grab anything you can carry from the box underneath it.''

He stepped into the swirling water, and rapidly inflated the Zodiac. They'd hit a sandbar. It was both a blessing and a curse, because, though it gave them a bit of dry ground to work with, it had also torn off the right wing of his plane.

Marisa, arms full, followed him, and he helped her from the plane, onto the bar, holding the cargo high, out of the water. ''Stay there.''

She nodded, looking ill. He wasn't surprised when her legs gave out, and he caught her before she fell back into the swirling river. ''I'm sorry,'' she mumbled, her hand pressed to her forehead. ''I'm so dizzy.''

He grabbed the duffel and stuffed it behind her. ''Lean against that. And don't let go. Can you swim?''

Marisa nodded weakly and sincerely hoped she wouldn't be called upon to actually do so. Every movement made her head swim. She curled her fingers into the black canvas of the bag with a death grip and drew her legs up the sandy surface, out of the water.

They'd crashed.

But they weren't dead.

She closed her eyes, aware of Tyler's rapid movements as he went back and forth between the boat he'd inflated and the plane.

Then he was talking to her, telling her to get in the small boat. She moved, feeling clumsy, and he ended up just lifting her over the side, tossing the duffel in after her.

She was shivering. The air felt colder than it ought to have for February. If she could just get warm...

Her fingers closed on the duffel and she fumbled for the zipper. He probably had clothes inside—

"What the hell are you doing?" He jerked the bag out of her hands and she'd have pitched forward onto her nose if he hadn't planted a hard hand on her shoulder first. "Stay out of there." He shoved the duffel as far away from her as it could go. Which wasn't far.

She didn't want to cry. She wouldn't cry. Not in front of him. "I'm cold."

"You're soaking wet. We both are. That, plus a

little shock.'' He shook his head and pulled a thin, silvery film from a small package. With a flick, he opened it out like a blanket and wrapped it around her shoulders. Then he tilted her head back and looked at her forehead. ''I'll get that cut taken care of in a minute,'' he said.

And Marisa's eyes flooded simply because his voice had been so gentle.

She was glad when he rolled out of the boat and headed back to the plane. She ducked her head and wiped her eyes. The nausea was subsiding. By the time he returned to the boat, she was sitting up, more or less steadily. He pushed the boat off the bar, walking alongside it until he was practically swimming. Then, with a slick motion, he slid over the side and flipped a small outboard into place. A moment later the motor was running with a reassuring sound.

But he didn't head up the river as she expected. Instead, after several yards, he let off on the throttle, leaving them to drift with the current. He was looking back at the crash, holding something in his hand. ''Cover your ears.''

Unthinkingly Marisa did as he bade. And then nearly jumped out of her skin at the short, sharp crack that blasted through the air when he pointed the small device and pressed a button.

She looked back. The front of the plane was engulfed in flames.

The front of the plane where the radio and all that wonderful, high-tech equipment was. She whirled on him. "How could you do that? What if they can't find us?"

"Who?"

Her teeth chattered with chills. "Whoever is g-going to rescue us!"

He'd opened the throttle of the outboard, and now they were moving fast down the river. "We are the ones doing the rescue. This is just a temporary hitch in the plans."

Marisa looked up at the afternoon sky. It seemed like hours had passed since the moment the plane had begun its tumble from the sky. But her logic told her it couldn't have been long at all. "I still don't see why you had to completely destroy the plane."

"Would you prefer the shooter to know that we got out alive? Or would you prefer him to find completely burned wreckage?"

She felt dread slice through her. How silly of her not to realize the person who'd shot at the plane might not be finished with them. "Why does El Jefe hate this Westin so badly?"

"Don't you know?"

She raked back the pieces of hair that had come loose from her chignon. "What do I have to do to convince you that I am not in league with El Jefe!"

She realized she was yelling, and closed her mouth with a snap.

"I'll let you know."

She shook her head, wincing at the pain in her face. At least her swimming head had cleared. And being wrapped like a hot dog in tin foil had done the trick of settling her chills. "You'd have been right in style with the witch trials," she told him.

For some reason, he found that amusing. His lip curled in an entirely unexpected and terribly brief grin.

Marisa looked away.

The river had narrowed from where they'd crashed to only about fifteen, perhaps twenty feet. The banks were steep, congested with heavy root growth from the trees that towered over them, nearly blocking out the sky above. As the small, tough boat skimmed steadily along the surface, Marisa couldn't help the feeling that she'd been left all alone in this world with a man whose smile could transform his face.

But a man who hated her, nonetheless.

She'd fallen asleep.

If she had a concussion, that wasn't a good thing. But Tyler was equally concerned about putting as much distance between them and the crash site as possible.

Still, he let off on the throttle. When she didn't stir, he reached for the black duffel bag and unzipped it. Inside were several other smaller containers, some locked closed, and he methodically checked each one, keeping an eye out for Marisa to stir. She didn't. And when he was satisfied that all of the contents had come through undamaged, he pulled out the first-aid kit and closed the bag once again.

Then he knelt beside her, freezing for a moment at the pain that seized his ribs. He waited, mentally counting off the seconds until he could breathe again. And when he could, he carefully pulled the loosened hair away from her forehead where she'd taken that gash.

The hair that had come free from her bun had dried into unruly waves and the slick black strands curled around his callused fingers with a gentle caress. He pulled away as if he'd been burned, and had to count off another few seconds until the pain eased. Then he just sat there, staring at her upturned face, while he called himself ten kinds of a fool.

Her lashes were long, thick. If she'd had any of that black stuff that women wore on them, it would have long worn off. Which meant they were naturally that soft and dark.

Her forehead was already turning a vivid shade of purple, but the cut wasn't as large as he'd first thought. More like the skin had simply split when she'd smacked her head against something during the impact.

He slowly unwrapped an antiseptic wipe as he studied her. Could she really be as innocent as her sleeping face suggested?

Without difficulty, he conjured a memory of Sonya. Even after he'd had his hands on evidence damning her for all eternity, she'd stared up at him, blue eyes wide as a child's.

He crumpled the foil wrapping from the moist wipe and tossed it onto the pile of stuff he'd salvaged from the plane. Dammit. He hated working with women.

Marisa jerked and gave a fretful moan as he dabbed her wound. When he smeared some ointment over it and pressed the adhesive bandage into place, she opened her eyes.

He was glad that they looked clear, steady. Her pupils were the same size, contracting equally against the lengthening sunlight.

He held up his hand. "How many fingers?"

"That's pretty rude." She pushed away his hand and the age old one-fingered salute. "And remarkably unimaginative." She ran her fingertips over the square bandage on her forehead. "I'm surprised you didn't leave it open to fester. Maybe I'd be taken with infection and then you could leave me to rot in the jungle.''

He sat back, sitting on the only plank of a seat the boat possessed. ''Who needs imagination? You've got more than enough for both of us.''

Marisa eyed him warily. He looked surprisingly at ease as he sat there, leaning over slightly, his arms resting on his wide-spread thighs, fingers loosely linked together. But then, he was part of some secret military group, so for all she knew, this was just a typical day on the job for him.

He possessed his share of scrapes, as well, mostly on his arms. One sleeve of his T-shirt was torn, baring the hard thrust of his shoulder, and he had smudges of what looked like grease down his chest.

She decided his arms were a safer focus than his chest. There were four or five thin scrapes down his right arm. A particularly nasty one circled down around his wrist. ''You should clean up your own cuts,'' she murmured.

Of course, being the big, macho military giant that he was, he made no move to do so. Rolling her eyes, she picked up the first-aid kit that was sitting by her feet and plucked through the contents until she found an antiseptic wipe. She tore it open and reached for his hand.

She didn't think too much about it, just swabbed the cloth firmly, rapidly, over the slash along his wrist. She turned his hand over and continued cleansing the cut. She knew the wipe had to sting furiously, yet he didn't so much as twitch.

His hands were remarkably graceful for such a large man. She'd have thought he'd have big, meaty palms and square fingers. But no. Sinew defined his tanned forearms, his wrists were well-shaped and his fingers long.

A vision of a well-manicured hand raised in anger accosted her and she stared, hard, at the hand she was tending, forcing the memory from her thoughts. Tyler's nails were clipped short, and calluses roughened his palms, as if he were more used to wielding a sword than a pen. If this man had ever subjected himself to a manicure, she'd eat her hat.

If she *had* a hat.

She suddenly pushed the wipe into his palm and sat back on her heels. Touching him hadn't been a good idea. He could finish cleaning his own scrapes.

Her clothes were no longer dripping water, but were distinctly damp and definitely uncomfortable. The items they'd taken from the plane were jumbled together beside her at the front of the boat. "Where's my suitcase?"

His eyebrows lifted. "Suitcase heaven?"

Her jaw dropped and she forgot all about the feel of his hands. "You managed to get all this." She shoved at the pile and something encased in a slick nylon bag slid off the top and landed by his boot. "But not my suitcase?"

"You'll live."

She wanted to hit him. So deep was the impulse, in fact, that she had to tuck her hands under her thighs to keep from doing so.

"Don't look so stricken," he drawled. "You're supposed to be a poor Mezcayan native. That doesn't extend to makeup and suits from Saks."

T-shirts and jeans for her sister and toys for the children. Books for her father and entertainment magazines for her mother. So many things that she'd collected to take into Mezcaya where she could talk Franco into delivering them for her to their family. She didn't like thinking of the items as a peace offering, though that may have been part of it. Mostly she had simply thought how much they might enjoy the items that they didn't ordinarily have. Things they couldn't obtain, or couldn't afford.

And now they were all gone. If they weren't destroyed by the water flooding the plane, they surely had been finished off by the charge that Tyler had set.

She hated the tears that burned behind her eyes and resolutely turned so that she didn't have to look at him. "Mezcayans don't arrive at *la Fortuna* wearing ruined linen suits, either," she said. His cammies wouldn't necessarily be out of place, but she'd stick out like a sore thumb.

"It's a long way from here to *la Fortuna*. We'll get clothes."

But she couldn't hope to replace the things that had been lost in her suitcase. Not now, not when she'd used the remainder of her meager savings on them. She sighed and furtively dashed away the tears.

She could find another reason for Franco to stop his madness, and she, herself, would begin again. Once she had her career back.

It was that reason she needed to remember. That reason she needed to focus upon. Tyler wasn't letting anything as minor as a plane crash get in the way of his plans. Neither would she.

"Here." He tossed a white bundle toward her and it landed on her lap. It was a T-shirt.

"I don't want to wear your shirt. I want to wear my own shirt."

"And people in hell want ice water. Your clothes are gone, princess."

"I am not likely to forget." The soft fabric crumpled in her fist. "Your clothes are wet, too."

"So?"

So, naturally, Mr. Macho could stand the discomfort, whereas she, Miss Princess, couldn't. "Turn around."

His lips twisted. "On a boat the size of a minute? Come on, M. After all—" his voice dropped hatefully "—we are supposed to be married."

As he watched her expression go from unbearably sad to angry, Tyler wondered if he'd hit a new low. All he knew was he was glad when Marisa's eyes went from liquid sadness to hot fury. If she was spitting mad, it was a lot easier to remember that he couldn't afford to trust her for a second.

If her expression was any indication, it *was* probably safer for him not to turn his back on her right now. Or he might find himself with a leather-shod foot being planted square in the center of it.

Her lips tightened and she lifted one slender hand to the top gold button on her suit. She flicked it free. And the next. The limp fabric sagged, displaying a narrow wedge of gold-toned curves and a glimpse of shining ivory fabric.

She wore a delicate gold chain. The cross at the base of it was minuscule. Her fingers touched the third button. Her eyes snapped with anger. He almost expected her to do it. To unfasten that third button.

Then she huffed. "Pig."

He didn't disagree with her.

She pivoted on her knees, facing away from him. She yanked off the jacket of her suit and swiftly tugged his T-shirt over her head. It caught on what remained of the knot at the back of her head, preventing her from sticking her head through. She muttered under her breath and pulled the shirt off once again to tear the pins out of her hair.

It slowly uncoiled, helped along by the breeze created by the boat as it skimmed the water, and sprang free into a riot of waves. She yanked the shirt over her head and flipped her hair loose.

Then she turned around to face him, her finely shaped features set into defiant lines. ''I hope you're satisfied.'' Her accent was more pronounced.

''I'm not even close to being satisfied, M. But when I am, you won't have any doubts about it.''

Three

Could a person go insane from being cooped in a boat that provided, possibly, eight by three feet of space? Most of which was taken up by a very long-legged, very annoying man?

Marisa thought that she very likely could. It seemed they'd been on the boat for hours, but she knew her sense of time was skewed. At least the T-shirt he'd given her was dry. She wished she could say the same about her slacks, socks and shoes.

Fortunately she was wearing relatively flat leather walking shoes. Unfortunately she didn't dare remove them lest they shrink as they dried, making her unable to wear them at all.

She pulled her fingers through her hair. It was unforgivably tangled now, thanks to being whipped into a mess by the breeze. She sat in the front of the boat facing Tyler. She caught her hair in her hand and held it down. "Do you—" She stopped to clear her throat. She would not be intimidated by a man, she reminded herself. "Do you really think it was El Jefe who shot at us?"

His hooded eyes studied her. "You tell me."

She bristled. "I've had enough of your implying I had something to do with this."

"I did more than imply it, M."

She swallowed. "You really do have quite an opinion of me."

He didn't bother to deny it.

"How can you even be sure the plane was shot? Maybe there was something else wrong with it."

"Believe me, I know."

Unease rippled through her and she turned to look over her shoulder in the direction they were traveling. The river was still narrow, highly congested in some places with boulders and reed, causing him to slow down to a crawl in order to maneuver the boat.

The small outboard droned on steadily, and though it was a comforting sound after the nightmare on the plane, it still sounded frightfully small in the vast silence around them. She sighed and turned toward him again. "Do you even know where we are?"

"I have a good idea."

Not that he would share the knowledge with her, she figured. Her head was throbbing and she scooted down more comfortably, stretching out her legs. She was careful to stay well away from him, however.

He leaned over, holding out a canteen. "Here. There's aspirin in the first-aid kit."

She hesitated, not sure she liked the way he seemed to read her mind. But common sense overruled, and she took the canteen, then found the packet of aspirin and swallowed them down. The water was cool and blessedly sweet and she wanted to guzzle it right down, but managed to refrain. She replaced the cap and handed it back to him. "Thank you."

His fingers brushed hers as he took the container and she sat back, rubbing her hand down her thigh.

"Trying to wipe away the germs?" He pulled off the lid and lifted the canteen to his mouth, drinking right where she had done.

Wipe away the tingling charge from his touch was more like it. "Yes, as a matter of fact, I was," she answered coldly. She shut her eyes. Crashing was exhausting work.

Eventually she felt him moving about in the minimal space in which there was to move. The motor was humming softly but they were doing little more than drifting in the congested water. She could hear him shifting the cargo, but kept her eyes resolutely shut.

When she heard a muttered oath cut short, however, she couldn't help but look to see what he was doing. He was sitting there, uncommonly still, head bowed, arms braced. Then he lifted his head, and she hastily closed her eyes again. The last thing she wanted him to do was find her studying him. Goodness only knew what he'd make of that.

Eventually the aspirin must have done the trick, for Marisa dozed off a little, and awoke only when she became aware of the sunlight, vivid and bright, on her face. She sat up, her muscles moving stiffly. While she'd slept, Tyler had secured the cargo beneath an odd sort of net. The river had widened, and they were fairly flying along the surface.

Her breath caught in her throat at the inescapably wild beauty of the landscape. Looking past Tyler, her gaze clung to the sight. This was the land of her birth. God, it had been so very long. She knew they had to be miles and miles away from the little mountainous piece of land her family had farmed for generations. But that didn't stop her from feeling a tug deep inside her.

"How long will it take for us to get there? To *la Fortuna?*" Maybe *she* wouldn't be going home, but if there was any chance at all that she could make sure that Franco *did,* she had to take it.

"Long enough." He was eyeing the river closely. "A week or so, on the outside. Assuming I've figured our location accurately enough."

She nodded. A week. She could handle that if she had to.

"Aren't you going to pitch a fit?"

Her eyebrows rose. "Should I?"

"Most women would."

She objected to that, but knew there was little point in saying so. He was just like Gerald. He would think whatever he chose to, regardless of the circumstances. It wouldn't matter whether he was miles away from the truth, or he—

"Hold on." Tyler's command was terse and it effectively jerked her out of her memories. "We're coming up on some rough water."

She whirled around to see the rapids were nearly upon them. "Rough?" She nearly choked. The water churned white and vicious among the rocks. "Why can't we—" She broke off the rest of the question. They couldn't go on land and carry the boat around the rapids because the banks on either side went nearly straight up. "I don't like traveling with you!" She curled her fingers around the hard, rubbery handles incorporated into the boat's design.

Tyler had already pulled in the outboard and was using the oar to help guide the suddenly rocking and plunging boat. Her heart rate escalated so fast that she felt dizzy with it. The roar of the water filled the air and she wondered why she hadn't been aware of it sooner. "What do I do?"

"Unless you want one really rough swim, stay in the boat."

She looked back at him, only to find his eyes lit with an unholy gleam. "You're enjoying this!"

His teeth flashed. "Gets the blood pumping, doesn't it?"

She frowned, then couldn't help the startled scream when the boat went into a nearly vertical plunge. One of Tyler's black bags—the one that he was nearly rabid about keeping near him—started to slide out from the net and she made a grab for it. She barely caught it with her fingertips even as she fell forward when the boat leveled for an all-too-brief moment. Water poured over the side and her arm felt nearly yanked out at the shoulder from where she still held on with one hand.

"What the hell are you doing? I told you to hold on!" Tyler's fingers dragged her back by the shirt.

"Then hold on to your own bloody bags! Ahh!" She shoved his precious black bag at him and was scrambling to get a good grip on the side of the boat once again. But it was too wet, too slippery, and the boat seemed to be free-falling again.

Tyler's fingers caught at Marisa's shirt, but he wasn't fast enough and like a rag doll tossed aside by a careless hand, she disappeared over the side of the inflatable. She screamed, her arms waving as the rough water dragged her under. Tyler cursed a blue streak, leaning over with the oar. "Grab it!"

She was close enough for him to see the terror in her eyes, close enough for him to hear her coughing as water clogged her nose and mouth, but not close enough for him to pull in.

He yelled at her again to grab the oar, could see that she was trying. But the boat was spinning one way and she the other. In the back of his mind was another boat, years ago that had capsized.

In an instant, he made the decision and pulled the oar in. He wasn't going to get to her. Not this way.

He ran a practiced eye over the riverbank, picked a spot heavy with overhanging trees. Muscles straining against the power of the ferocious water, using the oar as a rudder, he started inching the boat toward the spot. Before he could get close enough to the boulder-strewn bank to batter the inflatable to pieces, he dropped the oar and grabbed one of the tree branches, nearly getting ripped out of the boat as he fought the momentum of the river.

Hand over hand, legs wedged in the boat, he pulled through the churning water until he was past the worst of the rocks. With one hand wrapped around the thick branch, he grabbed the one duffel that he didn't dare lose, and heaved it far up onto the bank, scrambling up after it.

Free of its human anchor, the boat shot past the rocks, tearing off down the white, frothing water. He didn't spare a moment worrying about it, but ran after Marisa, slipping and sliding over the sharply inclined riverbank. "I'm Alpha Force, for crissakes," he muttered. "Not the flippin' Coast Guard."

Come on, Marisa. Open your eyes.

The voice seemed to come from a long way off. Marisa struggled against the weight in her chest. Maybe, despite her sins, God had invited her to heaven after all.

You're okay. Come on, baby, that's it. Breathe.

She coughed. Her lungs burned, her throat was on fire. She coughed again and felt her head being tilted as water dribbled past her lips.

"Good girl."

It was Tyler, she realized weakly. Most assuredly not The Father. She started to speak, but couldn't as she coughed up more water.

"Shh. Take it easy. We're not going anywhere just now."

She forced her eyelids up, looking at him through her water-spiked lashes. He was soaked to the skin, too. *"No soy muerto."*

"Yeah, that's it. *Muerto.* Not *muerto.* Definitely not *muerto.*" He smoothed her hair away from her face. "You're not dead. You're gonna be all right. Just rest."

Closing her eyes was a relief. The coughing spasms began to slow. Only then the shivers began. And she felt his presence leave for a moment, but then he was back and she recognized the crinkling sound of that silver blanket as he wrapped her in it and pulled her right onto his lap, holding her close there on the bank of that deceptively peaceful river.

He was so warm. So solid.

He made no annoying comments. No accusations that she'd brought the incident down upon herself through her own stupidity. He didn't shift her around as if he couldn't wait to get her away from him. He didn't try to cop a feel.

He didn't do anything but hold her securely, until the shudders racking her body started to ease.

Tears slid from the corners of her eyes.

And even then, still, he held her.

Eventually the world seemed to calm again. She felt the afternoon sun on her face. Heard the steady rush of the river, like wind through the leaves, and the chatter of the birds in the trees. The moment she moved, Tyler was settling her away from him, pushing himself to his feet and heading over to the boat that was tugging, innocent as a babe, against the mooring line.

She chalked up the sense of loss to shock.

He tossed that duffel of his—the one she'd ended up going overboard because of—under the net in the boat, then uncapped the canteen and threw back his head, his strong brown throat working as he drank deeply.

He finished, and looked at her, holding the canteen aloft.

She made a face.

"Didn't think so," he deadpanned.

Then he came back for her and helped her into the boat once more before pushing off into the river that seemed as quiet as if it had never tried to suck her into its depths.

Marisa started to tremble again and she huddled deeper in the silver blanket. "I don't understand." Her teeth were chattering. "Why d-d-didn't you leave me?"

"Don't get too excited," he muttered, slicking his own wet hair back with one hand. "I expect you to prove useful before too long."

She was so exhausted, she couldn't even take offense. She laid her head back against the duffel bag behind her. "If we manage to live l-l-long enough to g-get to *la Fortuna*."

The fact that he didn't respond to that was of no comfort whatsoever. He just started up the outboard again, and the boat picked up speed.

Though he'd feel better if they put as much distance between them and the crash site as possible, Tyler knew that Marisa had pretty much reached the end of her rope.

He could actually see the shivers racking her

body. She needed dry clothes, food and a solid piece of land under her feet.

If he were alone, he'd have kept onward. But he wasn't alone. And for all he knew, their current, less-than-optimal situation was her fault, anyway. It was only a stroke of luck that the inflatable had gotten wedged between two sharp rocks not far from where he'd finally reached Marisa. The cargo net had even kept most of their gear from being swept down the river.

Marisa had been pretty wedged, too. Her hair had been caught in a tangle of fallen trees. He wasn't sure if she'd caught the nearly submerged branches deliberately in an effort to save herself, or if her hair had done the job. In either case, she'd been face-down and blue when he'd finally gotten her untangled and dragged her from the water. But he had found her and he had gotten her breathing again.

He studied the shoreline but it was nearly an hour before he found something to his liking. Marisa was still huddled there, but he knew she wasn't asleep. He carefully directed the boat into the heavily sheltered inlet, finally cutting the motor altogether. He had to push aside overgrown vines and fronds to make room for the small inflatable, and when they were through, he made sure they fell back into place. As a blind, it was a pretty effective one, and once he pulled the boat onto shore, nobody from the river would be able to see them.

"Good thing I'm not claustrophobic." Marisa sat up and shrugged off the emergency blanket. Her voice was husky, as if her throat was still raw from the water she'd exhaled.

"Yeah," Tyler agreed. He forced his gaze away from her and slid over the side of the boat to finish pushing it up on the shore. Marisa clambered over the side before he could assist her. He saw her take a few steadying steps, then eye the bushes.

"Don't go far, and watch out for snakes."

She looked like she might be embarrassed, but managed to cover it pretty well as she ducked beneath a heavy tree branch and disappeared into the thick growth.

Tyler raked his hands through his hair and grabbed the duffel containing his clothes and tossed it up on the ground. First thing he needed to do was get her some dry clothes, because watching her walk around in a T-shirt made transparent in its soaked state was going to kill him.

He had cleared a space on the bank when she returned. Telling himself he wouldn't, he still looked at her. He could have told her not to bother plucking self-consciously at the shirt the way she was. When he'd pulled her out of the water, he'd seen about as much as there was to see without her being nude.

Which was maybe what he should think now. Because there was nothing at all erotic about holding in your arms a woman who looked half-dead.

"There are some dry clothes there for you. And insect repellent. Use it." He knew his voice sounded rough and annoyed. He lifted his chin toward the line he'd stretched between two branches. "Spread out your wet stuff. If we're lucky, they'll be dry by morning." Stained beyond belief by the mud they'd both picked up in the river, but hopefully dry enough to wear again.

She was silent as she picked up the pile of clothes and the bottle of repellent and disappeared again behind the trees. He almost wished she'd made some smart-ass comment. It would have told him that she was bouncing back to normalcy.

The flame was crackling, easily licking through the collection of dried twigs before it could bite into the larger pieces of tree branch. When he straightened, he unconsciously cradled an arm around his aching rib cage for support.

"What's wrong?"

He jerked around, cursing under his breath at the pain that stabbed through him. He hadn't heard her make a sound as she emerged from the bushes, yet there she was. Wearing another one of his T-shirts and a pair of roughly woven peasant-style trousers that he'd brought along for himself. She'd taken the hem of the off-white pants and tied them up in little knots. It was effective enough at keeping the too-long length from tripping her. She'd also rolled up the short sleeves of the T-shirt, and knotted the hem at her hip. She looked entirely at home in the jungle, in fact. Except for the leather shoes she wore, which would've looked more at home on a yuppie Wall Street broker.

"Mr. Murdoch?" She spoke to him, but he noticed she didn't exactly look at him. "Is something wrong?"

"Other than what's already gone wrong?" He blew out a breath. So, she could move silently when she wanted to. It didn't have to mean anything. "Lose the 'mister', would you?"

She murmured something he couldn't quite catch, and finished hanging her wet clothes over the line, then moved closer to the fire.

"Think you can eat something?"

Marisa fingered the ragged edge of the bandage on her forehead. She couldn't believe it hadn't come off completely when she'd gone overboard. Tyler had dragged a fallen piece of tree closer to the fire, obviously using some of the smaller pieces to feed the flame. She sat down on the far end of the log and pressed the adhesive bandage back into place for about the hundredth time. "At this point, I think

I could eat the bark off this tree stump,'' she admitted tiredly.

He made a soft sound; almost a laugh, but not quite. ''I think we can do a little better than that.''

She finally just tugged off the loose bandage and tossed it into the small flame. ''Tell me what to do.''

''Stay inside the boat.''

She blinked, then felt a reluctant smile tug at her lips. ''Very funny. The only reason I wasn't holding on was that I was trying to keep *that* from going over.'' She pointed at the small black bag of his. Even now, he'd set it carefully aside, away from the fire, away from the water. ''What have you got in there, anyway? A gun?''

''I don't carry a weapon.''

That startled her. ''Yet you intend to go into *la Fortuna*?''

''I'd hardly go in as a domestic packing something. They undoubtedly search everyone who enters.''

''How are you going to get your Westin free? I would certainly think that his guards *do* have weapons.''

''I'm sure they do, too.''

''And?'' She waited for him to say something, anything, about how he intended to overcome armed guards, then felt annoyance bubble inside her. ''Never mind. Of course you can't tell me anything.

I've probably got some secret transmitter glued to one of my molars that I'll use to relay your plans to my partners, the El Jefe.'' Her voice dropped sarcastically. She didn't expect a response, so she wasn't surprised when she received none. "Is it just me, or do you simply detest all women?''

At that, he did look at her, and she wished that she'd kept her mouth shut.

"Oh, princess,'' he murmured, "I like women just fine.''

There was no mistaking his meaning and she hated the curl of awareness that slipped through her. "But not me. What is it? You have something against Latinas?''

"You could be from Mars and I wouldn't care. I don't work with women.''

"So you're not a racist, just a chauvinist.''

He shrugged, obviously unperturbed. "Since I'm such a chauvinist, maybe I should let *you* rustle up some grub.''

She'd called Gerald a chauvinist. And worse. Every name had been true. And he'd been apoplectic with rage.

Tired of the comparisons, and definitely not willing to leave her fate in a man's hands—even for something as prosaic as food—she pushed to her feet. But the abrupt movement made her head swim, and she swayed unsteadily.

"Whoa." Tyler caught her and nudged her back down to the fallen log. "Come on, princess, just sit, would you? I've got enough to do without scraping you up off the dirt."

Since she felt more than a little nauseated all of a sudden, she decided to do just that. She propped her head gingerly on her palms and closed her eyes. How many times had she thought herself to be exhausted working at the restaurant for a full shift only to work for hours more on an interpreting project? Those days were a snap compared to falling out of the sky and shooting the rapids.

"Here."

She looked up to see Tyler holding out the canteen again. He also dropped a foil-wrapped protein bar on her lap. "That'll keep you going until I can get something else started. But I'll warn you. You might prefer the tree bark. And with the water you swallowed, you might not feel too great when you do eat."

She turned the bar over in her fingers. "You're a puzzle, Mr. Murdoch."

"Tyler. And don't bother trying to put it together," he said as he stepped down to the water's edge and dropped in the fishing line he'd managed to rig while she wasn't watching. "There are too many pieces missing."

He hunkered down on his heels, at that moment

looking more like he'd been carved from stone than flesh and blood. He'd fished her out of the roiling river, tended her cuts, and made sure she had dry clothes.

He'd held her until she'd stopped shaking.

All this from a man who freely admitted he neither trusted her, nor wanted her presence on this excursion.

A puzzle, indeed. One that disturbed her in ways she didn't even want to examine.

The only light came from the dancing glow of the fire that Tyler kept burning. It wasn't likely to get terribly cold that night; she knew, because they were still at a fairly low elevation. But the fire would keep any curious critters from getting too close, and as far as Marisa was concerned, that was a good thing.

After Tyler had cooked the fish he'd snared, he'd flipped out a tarp and made a quick shelter with it and a length of rope and some rocks before tossing a bedroll under it for Marisa. She'd been so grateful to lie on something other than the rich, moist dirt under their feet that she could have kissed him.

She started to look at the watch on her wrist, but remembered that she'd lost it somewhere along the way from the plane to this small indent off the river. Beyond the shelter and the canopy of trees overhead, she could just barely make out the pinprick of a few stars. And beyond the circle of the fire, she could hear the occasional rustle of leaves.

Other than whatever animals were making their nighttime rounds, they were utterly alone. And still, Tyler sat at the fire, looking very much as if he were on guard.

If she'd had any doubts that the reason the plane had gone down was because they'd been shot at, they were thoroughly dispelled by the disturbing sight of Tyler at watch.

She lay there for a long while, watching him from her vantage point in the darkness. He'd been studying a map earlier, and now it was rolled up in a narrow tube, sitting on the ground beside him. Right beside the machete that gleamed in the firelight.

She *should* be scared out of her wits. But while she was very definitely uneasy, Marisa couldn't actually say that she was frightened. Neither by Tyler, nor by whatever dangers may be following them.

If Tyler had truly wanted to be rid of her, he'd had the opportunity more than once. Even well before the rapids, he could have left the airport without her. Somehow, she just couldn't envision anyone chasing after Tyler for disregarding his orders to cooperate with the other parties involved in his rescue operation. Yet he'd kept her with him right from the start.

The start. It seemed ridiculous that it had been less than twenty-four hours ago.

Sighing quietly, she rolled to her feet, wincing at the aches and pains that were, thankfully, all that remained from her river dunking. Then she soundlessly crept into the bushes and relieved herself.

But before she could slip back to the bedroll, she heard the snap of a twig and felt an arm wrap, hard, around her neck.

"Where do you think you're going?" Tyler's voice was nearly soundless next to her ear.

She kicked back at his shin and felt some small satisfaction at the grunt he gave when her hard shoe connected. *"El idiota terco,"* she rasped. "Stubborn idiot! Let me go."

The pressure on her neck lifted fractionally. "Tell me."

"I was using nature's lavatory." She kicked him again, harder this time. "Now let me go!" Her demand was loud enough to startle something in the trees into flight. She followed it up with a hard jab of her elbow into his ribs.

He let her go so abruptly she pitched forward, falling onto her hands and knees. She rose, brushing her stinging palms against her thighs. "What is wrong with you? Don't ever sneak up on me like that again!"

"Calm down."

"You calm down! What's the matter? Were you afraid I was going to sneak up on you and slit your throat or something?" She was aware of his shape, hunched forward at the waist, as she stomped over the leaf-laden ground and sat down on the bedroll under the shelter.

Her heart was beating like a mad hornet and she deliberately calmed herself. If she'd hurt him with her elbow, it was no more than he deserved. The self-defense instructor had thoroughly drilled that principle into the participants of the class she'd taken a few years ago.

He rounded the tarp, still with that odd, sort of hunched posture, and she watched him go over to the log and slowly lower himself onto it.

He saved your life.

So what? He grabbed you from behind!

But...

Stop feeling guilty!

Her teeth worried the inside of her lip as her mental debate continued. "Tyler—"

"Go back to sleep."

Definitely stop feeling guilty. She lay back on the mat and pulled the thin blanket over herself. "Yes, *sir.*"

Once Tyler was sure Marisa had fallen back asleep, he managed to pull his own shirt over his head. He'd broken his ribs once, and was still pretty sure he hadn't done that much damage in the crash. But the rest of the day's activities—not the least of which was Marisa's wicked little elbow move— hadn't helped any. He ran his fingertips gingerly over himself. No broken skin, nothing but one huge ache.

Forcing himself to move, he downed one of the precious-few aspirin from the first aid kit and yanked the T-shirt off the line to get it wet again. Then he folded up the cool, wet cloth and pressed it against his side. The pitch-dark corner beneath the tarp beckoned, but he ignored it and stretched out by the fire, glad for the warmth as the temperature had dropped considerably.

There were only a few hours left before daybreak, and no matter what disasters had occurred that day, their trek would have to continue the next.

Westin's life depended on it.

Four

"You know, if we're lost, you might as well just say so."

Tyler rolled up the map again and stuffed it inside his pack. "We're not lost."

"Then why do we seem to be going in circles?"

"We're not. We're just not where we're supposed to be." An understatement of the year.

Marisa's eyes rolled. As far as Tyler was concerned, she'd more than adequately recovered from the ordeal the day before. Her tongue was certainly back in fighting form. Since dawn, she'd been full of questions that he wouldn't answer and comments that he'd mostly ignored.

Quick as a thief, she plucked out the map and scooted back onto the bench as she unrolled it. They were on the river—mercifully calm—and the sun had been climbing over the edge of the horizon for only a few hours.

"Where are we supposed to be, then?" She was peering at the map.

He sighed and flipped the map around so that she

was looking at it right-side-up. "You say you speak how many languages?"

She sniffed, and somehow—despite the bruised cut on her forehead, the dirt-smudged clothes, and the hair that had worked into wild ringlets during the night—she managed to look down her nose at him. "More than you," she said, her lips twitching. "Would you rather I had stellar map-reading abilities than fluency in Mezcayan?"

He jabbed his finger on the map. "There."

"Mmm." She pushed his hand away. "*There* is a mountain range with no river in sight." She made a production of looking around them. "And we are very clearly on a river. A river I have no particular love for, I might add."

"We won't be on it for long," he said flatly. He figured the gas for the outboard might hold out for the rest of that day. Mostly, though, he wanted to get off the river where he felt uncomfortably like a sitting duck. But he didn't really want to tell Marisa that he strongly suspected they were being tracked.

Not until he knew by whom.

"We're down here somewhere, aren't we?" She was tracing her slender finger along a winding blue line. "Heading—" she squinted up at the sky— "east, more or less. But isn't *la Fortuna* northwest from here?"

"Yeah." There was no point in denying the obvious.

She looked like she wanted to ask more, but she didn't. She just rolled up the map and put it away. Then she leaned against her elbows and shook back her long hair, lifting her face to the sun. She'd seemed nervous when he'd first loaded them up in the boat, but that had obviously passed. "Some yacht you've got here."

"Nothing but the best for the boys of the United States military."

Her soft lips curved slightly. "When I was a little girl, I dreamed about riding in a boat with a real motor." She sighed deeply, her amber eyes hidden by her lashes. "I didn't even know what a yacht looked like until I left Mezcaya."

"Right."

Her chin lowered and she looked at him. "What is that supposed to mean?"

"Don't tell me you didn't grow up with the best your country had to offer."

Her eyebrows lifted. "Okay, I won't." She leaned back again, looking for all the world like a woman sunning herself on the decks of the fictitious yacht.

"You're going to get sunburned." He rummaged in the first aid kit and found a narrow tube of sunblock. The weather couldn't be more perfect right now, with the rainy season still weeks off and the temperatures mild. But he could already see her nose was getting pink, and the last thing he wanted to do was have to nurse her through some wicked sunburn.

"No more than you will." But she took the tube and carefully rubbed some into her face and over her bare arms. Then she jackknifed forward and started smearing the stuff on him.

He jerked back.

"Oh, cut it out, Murdoch, and sit still. I'm not going to poke out your eyes."

"Last night I was Tyler."

She sniffed, looking bored. She was so close to him that he could see the rim of darker brown in her irises, and the flecks of gold that gave them that amber glow. "Last night I felt bad for trying to put my elbow through to your spine after you'd saved my life."

"You did a fair job of it, too," he muttered, finally pulling away and taking the tube from her to finish the job himself. It just wasn't a good idea to be too close to her, to feel her hands on him. "Where'd you learn to do that, anyway?" He'd had her in a damn secure hold, yet she'd managed to defend herself pretty well even after the day she'd had.

Her shoulder lifted, and she suddenly seemed inordinately interested in the passing riverbank. "Did you know why those trees there are called strangler figs? They're parasites. The roots choke out the newer host trees.'' The smooth line of her jaw tightened. "I took a course once.''

"Botany or self-defense?"

She didn't answer. "What if we hit more rapids today?"

"Stay in the boat."

Her lips twisted. "Oh, that just gets funnier every time you say it, Murdoch."

"A course. Not a class."

She shook her head slightly. "What does it matter to you?"

"Just want to know how adept you might be at—"

"At what?" Her eyes went hot and angry. "Disarming you?" She tossed up her arms. "What on earth did I ever do to make you so terribly trusting of me?"

She was disarming. Only not in the way she was referring. And he finally acknowledged what had been tugging at the back of his mind since he first laid eyes on her. She reminded him of Haley. Haley Mercado.

It wasn't just the way Marisa had gone over the side of the boat that made him aware of the similarities, either. It was her looks, her spirit and that damnably appealing hint of vulnerability that she seemed hell-bent on hiding.

It was so many years ago that it seemed like another lifetime when Tyler had been half in love with Haley, though she'd never thought more of him than as a friend of her brother's. And she'd died in that other lifetime. In a boating accident that he still felt guilty about.

If he, Luke, Spence and Flynt hadn't been three sheets to the wind from celebrating their freedom and return from the Gulf, they'd never have encouraged Haley to go on that midnight boat ride with them, and she'd have never even been in the vicinity when their boat capsized.

It'd been two weeks before her poor body was discovered. And until Sonya came along, Tyler hadn't let himself get remotely close to caring for another female. Oh, there were women in his life. Ones who came and went, who'd share their bodies and a laugh or two before Tyler headed on down the road. His unwilling attraction to *this* woman was nothing more than those nearly forgotten feelings he'd had for a sweet girl from back home who'd died much too young. It was the only explanation.

There'd been nothing sweet about Sonya, though. She'd been as focused on their missions as he'd been. Or so he'd thought until she'd betrayed him. Betrayed her country.

Sonya had taught him two things. First, that love might be real enough for some, but for him, it was not. And secondly, that working with women only led to disaster.

Marisa watched Tyler's expression. She didn't know who or what he was thinking about, and thought that was probably a good thing. Because a colder expression than she'd ever seen had come over his face.

"I took a self-defense course because I never wanted a man to sneak up behind me and grab me in a choke-hold again," she said evenly. Then she turned to face forward. He could make of that what he wanted. She had no intention of explaining any further.

"Someone hurt you." His voice was flat.

Marisa shrugged. Over the years, she'd learned to do that when she thought about what Gerald had done. But hurt was too mild a word. He'd ruined her.

"And you don't want to talk about it," Tyler concluded.

"I thought men didn't like to do all that talking stuff that we women are so fond of."

"Talkin's okay." His drawl was dry as dust. "Unless there's somethin' more entertaining to do. And between men and women, there's usually something more entertaining to do."

"How profound."

"Hey, darlin', I'm a Texas boy. We're full of profundity."

"You're definitely full of something." She hid her reluctant smile. A man more removed from a "boy" she'd never before seen. She realized he was heading the boat toward the bank again. "Are we stopping?"

"I want to go up that hill there and get a look-see around."

Her jaw loosened a little as she looked up at the "hill." It would take them hours to scale that peak. "Something you're hoping to see when you get to the top?"

"When *we* get to the top, yes."

"But you're not going to tell me," she finished for him. "You're so predictable, Murdoch."

"That's me," he agreed as he climbed over the side of the boat and pulled it up onto the bank. "Predictable as the sunrise."

She got out, too, and helped him drag the inflatable farther into the trees where it couldn't be seen at all.

Then he was flipping a small daypack on his back and strapping the machete onto his belt. He tossed her a canteen. It was barely half full, though he had another. And he'd disinfected some water the night before with some special tablets he'd had with him.

She took a drink, then mirroring him, slid the strap crosswise over her shoulder.

It was getting steamy and warm, though the temperature was probably no higher than the mid-seventies. Once they headed deeper into the forest, it would be cooler, though no less humid. She tugged fruitlessly at her hair, wishing she had a comb or an elastic band. Anything to get it out of her face and off her neck. "I'm gonna cut it off," she told herself.

"What? Your hair?" Apparently satisfied that he'd secured the boat and the rest of their stuff as safely and unobtrusively as he could, he brushed past her and headed into the close-set trees. "I nearly had to do that to get you untangled from the trees in the river. Would have been a shame, though."

Her hands paused on her hair, then she hurriedly finished knotting it back and followed after him. "Did my ears deceive me or did you almost give me a compliment just then?"

"Stating a fact, M. That's all. You've got great hair."

She made a face at his back. "Silly me."

She thought she heard him laughing softly, but knew she had to be imagining it.

Within minutes, the path that Tyler was forging headed sharply upward. The machete was much more than an affectation; he had to hack his way steadily through the growth and as Marisa followed him, the steady swipe and thwack of the blade melded into a mesmerizing rhythm.

She wasn't even aware that she was humming beneath her breath until Tyler stopped short and looked back at her. "What are you singing?"

She blinked. "What? Oh." Her face flushed. "Just something that my *abuela* sang when my father was working in the field."

"Field?"

"Generally that's what a farmer does."

He turned smoothly and led the way once more. "What'd he grow? Starbucks coffee?"

She couldn't have been more pleased when a branch that he'd just pulled out of his way bounced back and rapped him hard on the butt. Nearby, two birds were startled into flight, their striking yellow, red and white feathers looking vivid against the world of green around them. "You're a snob," she stated.

"Hardly. I just don't believe you grew up on one of the little farms that dot Mezcaya's landscape."

"But you'll believe I'm somehow in league with El Jefe. Are all Texans as pigheaded as you, or am I just particularly blessed with your company?"

"You're blessed."

She huffed, and they trudged onward.

It seemed to take forever. Marisa realized she was counting every footstep, and made herself stop, because that just seemed to add to the agony screaming through her thighs and calves.

She'd thought she was in fairly decent physical condition, but this was making her seriously doubt it. Just putting one foot in front of the other grew to be a mammoth task and she could feel blisters forming on her heels, despite the thick cotton socks of his that she wore.

Tyler, however, didn't look as if he were suffering in the least from anything, much less leather shoes that were shrinking. The daypack looked small where it hung below his broad shoulders. The only indication that he was feeling any effort at all over the hike was the perspiration streaking down the back of his olive drab shirt. Considering the humidity, however, a person could sweat like that from standing still.

When she realized she was also watching the way his camouflage pants hugged his rear as they climbed upward, she looked back along the path they'd made, but it was nearly impossible, even with the swath he was cutting, to see exactly where they'd passed through. Everywhere she looked they were surrounded by trees. New growth that was striving mightily to get past the palms and monstrously huge ferns that grew closer to the ground. Old growth that was being eaten away by moss or insects. Even looking straight up, all she could see was the canopy of forest over her. And all she could hear was a cacophony of sound.

Fumbling with the canteen, she took a long drink. She was a native of this land, yet she could do nothing but yearn for wide-open spaces where the sky was visible no matter where you were and the wild foliage didn't seem ready to overtake anything or anybody who made the mistake of standing still for longer than a minute or two at a time. And if that didn't get you, then one misstep of the foot could put you in a wash where the soil had been wiped away by one of the rains. And then there were the snakes...

"Need a break?"

She realized Tyler was waiting several yards ahead and capped the canteen as she shook off her silliness. "No." She set her chin and determinedly walked forward. "Let's just get this done."

But he didn't move, not even when she caught up to him, and she wanted to put her hands on his chest and shove him out of the way. Either that, or put her hands on his chest and just lie there, resting, for about a month.

Which was most definitely an unacceptable, ludicrous notion. Just because she now knew exactly how solid and strong that chest felt beneath her cheek. "If I stop I won't get going again," she admitted breathlessly. "Now move, would you?"

"We're almost there."

She snorted. "How can you tell?"

"You're doing great."

Encouraging words from him did nothing to alleviate her mounting discomfort. But arguing the point simply took too much energy. So she focused on watching his feet, reminded herself what was at stake and kept walking.

And then, they were there.

As if the world was a flower that had suddenly opened its petals to the sun, they were out of the suffocating, close forest.

"You can see forever," she breathed, turning in a slow circle.

Only it wasn't entirely true. The summit was draped like an elegant lady in layers of silken, wispy clouds. And while the trek up had been filled with the noises of the forest, now it seemed oddly quiet.

Otherworldly.

Tyler watched Marisa's face as she stared off into the distance, and wondered what she was thinking to cause that look of melancholy. He knew she was exhausted. Hell, his chest felt as if it was on fire. Yet, she hadn't complained, not once, and he'd made no concessions to her in the hike.

"It's quite a view," he finally admitted, mentally kicking himself for not being sure which view he was referring to. Marisa, or the richly carpeted peaks and valleys stretching out below them.

Her gaze slid his way, and her expression was no longer sad. Instead her eyes seemed lit from something deep inside her. "It's kind of exhilarating, don't you think?"

"Feeling like you're literally on top of the world?"

She smiled. "Yes. Exactly." Then she seemed to shake herself a little and her smile disappeared. "All right, we're at the top. Are you getting what you need from your little look-see?"

"What's the matter? In a hurry to go back down?"

The thought seemed to horrify her, though she didn't say so. He flipped open the daypack to pull out two protein bars. He handed her one, then took out his map.

"They taste better the hungrier you are," Marisa observed as she eagerly bit into her bar and sat down, cross-legged, in the overgrown grass that covered the mountaintop.

"You'd be surprised what can taste great in comparison to starving," he murmured absently as his mind calculated distances and travel time. In the Gulf, thanks to a tiny batch of unstable explosives that went off in his gear at the most inopportune time, he and his friends had been captured and held hostage for weeks. They'd have starved to death if not for Westin's actions to rescue them. Dirt wasn't exactly high nutrition.

He pulled out the small binoculars and scoped out the terrain that was—hallelujah—still visible through the thickening clouds thanks to the powerful lenses. When he was satisfied with his bearings, as well as the fact that whoever was on their tail—if, in fact, it wasn't some innocent person out for a little exploration—was still far behind them, he stiffly lowered himself to the ground and stretched out flat on his back, stifling a sigh. Then he peeled open his protein bar.

Five minutes and they would need to get going again.

Marisa's arm stretched out above her. "It's almost as if you could touch heaven with your fingertips up here," she said in a hushed voice.

"If there is one."

She folded her arms around her knees. "I suppose you don't believe in heaven or hell."

"Hell is real enough."

"Yes," she murmured after a moment. "It is."

It was only curiosity, he told himself, that finally got the better of him. "Who was it?" As far as Tyler was concerned, it took the heinous actions of another person to put that particular look in someone's eyes.

She understood exactly what he meant. But it was

a while before she finally answered, as if she were as reluctant to answer the question as he'd been to pose it. "My ex-fiancé."

He wasn't terribly surprised at that, though she still seemed too young to have fit so much into her life.

"And you?" She barely waited a beat. "No, wait. It was undoubtedly a woman. One you had to work with, I'll bet." Her lips twisted. "You're a puzzle, Murdoch, but those pieces are obvious even to an untrustworthy Latina like me."

"I told you I don't give a flip what your heritage is. At least you know what it is."

"And you don't know yours?"

"I know enough to know what you make of your life is up to you, not your parents, or lack of 'em." Annoyed with the direction things were headed, annoyed that he'd wanted to know who had hurt her, he pushed to his feet. And barely held back a vicious oath as his ribs protested.

"What's wrong?"

"Nothing." He stuffed the empty wrappers in his pack and shouldered it again. "Let's move."

"Nothing," she mimicked under her breath as she fiddled for a moment with her shoes before standing. Tyler set off down the trail he'd created on their way up, and praying that she still had some skin left on her heels when their jaunt was over, she followed.

The forest had barely begun to thicken again into that enclosed verdant world when a low murmur of thunder rolled through the sky. It was the only warning they had before fat raindrops began sneaking through the leaves to plop on them.

"Perfect," she heard Tyler mutter.

"Give it five minutes," she told his back. "It'll pass. At least it's not the rainy season. That's when you have sunlight for five minutes before it passes."

Only, five minutes passed and the rain showed no sign of letting up. Tyler gave her one telling look over his shoulder before he continued hacking his way downward.

Five minutes became fifty.

The ground grew slick. Her leather-soled shoes lost what little traction they'd had and she had to catch herself, more than once, from falling on her rear. When she actually slipped far and fast enough to bump into Tyler, she'd begun to think that sliding down the mountain on her rear might just be easier.

He caught her while she steadied herself. "We've gotta do something about those shoes of yours."

She started to comment on that.

"I know, I know. Don't start." He ran his dark gaze down her. "I suppose you had hiking boots in that suitcase of yours."

She hadn't, but she couldn't resist letting him feel

some compunction for having blown up her belongings, so she let him think what he liked.

They set off again, Tyler moving even more slowly, because of her shoes, she was sure. She was wet, muddy, and the sustenance from the protein bar had only gone so far. "I had toys and clothes and magazines and books," she said, her irritation with the entire situation audible in her tone.

"Pardon?"

"In the suitcase. I'd planned to have them sent to my family." Only she knew that even if he had saved them from the plane, she couldn't actually see them carting the weighty objects all over the countryside.

Tyler frowned. Delivered? "Why not take 'em yourself?"

She didn't answer, and his boot slipped in the mud when he looked back at her. That would have been fine, if not for Marisa, who didn't slow up quickly enough. She skidded and bumped him, her arms flailing as she fought for balance.

Resignation swept through him in the millisecond before they both went down, arms and legs tangling as they gained momentum. He barely caught a glimpse of Marisa's horrified face before mud splashed over them both.

Then he instinctively wrapped his arms around her, shoved her face down against his chest, and

went with the flow. At least he was headed downward feetfirst, he thought, as the ground seemed to
turn into one giant mud slide. His boots broke off
the worst of the foliage that wasn't washed away by
mud. A good thing, because the world was a blur of
bumps and turns and the only thing he had some
measure of control over was hanging on to the be-
draggled, shapely woman lying on top of him.

They shot out from the trees, Tyler grimly aware
that they were nowhere near where they'd left the
inflatable, and he dug his heels into the earth, determined to keep them from sliding right off the riverbank and back into the water.

Crushing Marisa to his chest with one arm, he
caught out at anything they passed with the other,
slowing their descent even more.

Finally. They bumped and rolled and slid to a
bone-jarring stop, his boots mere inches from the
water's edge.

Marisa was shaking. Tyler could feel every quake
through to his bones. Moving gingerly, afraid of
where she might be hurt, he gently rolled her to the
side, leaning over her. He peeled back a river of
silky black hair. Her eyes were closed, her mouth
parted as she gasped for air. Mud covered her cheeks
and he brushed some of it away, only succeeding in
leaving a smear from his own caked hands.

"Come on, Marisa," he murmured. "It's over. It's okay."

Then she opened her eyes, still quaking.

And laughed.

He sat back like a shot, skidding an inch closer to the water.

Her hands pressed to her stomach and she bent over, shaking with laughter. He shook his head, feeling a chuckle himself.

When she tried to wipe her face with the hem of the shirt, leaving it only dirtier, she laughed even harder, startling a monkey from the branches overhead into swinging even higher where it let out an ungodly howl.

Marisa rolled onto her hands and knees, pushing herself up until she could stand over him. "Life with you is definitely not boring, Murdoch," she finally acknowledged, still breathless with laughter. "And here I'd just been thinking it would be faster to get down here on our rear ends."

He looked up at her, and felt a sudden shaft of arousal so fierce it left him aching. "You're not hurt."

She ran her hands through her tangled hair, scattering droplets of muddy water. "Well, you are a bit too hard to pass for a pillow, but I'd say you took the worst of it."

His lips twisted. She had no idea just how unpillowlike he was. He pushed to his feet, yanking off the daypack, keeping his back to her. ''Are you always this accident prone, or is it only with me that sh—stuff like this happens?'' If he'd hoped to annoy her, he failed. For she just went off into another peal of laughter as she looked up the mountain they'd just descended in record time.

''Only with you, apparently,'' she managed to say between giggles. ''You're blessed.''

He fought a laugh, thinking she must be contagious. She sure as hell was a confounding creature.

He'd wiped as much mud from the daypack as he could, but the only thing that would get it remotely clean would be the river. He flipped it open. The map was toast, but that didn't concern him as much as the contents of the small case at the bottom of the pack. The small supply of explosives he was carrying was extremely stable, but the transmitter was another matter.

''Of course, *now* it stops raining. I feel as if I have mud in places I didn't know I had,'' Marisa admitted, as she sat on the edge of the water and stuck her feet right in, shoes, socks and all.

Thinking about any place on her body was a stupid activity. Telling himself so didn't prevent him from doing just that, though. While she was leaning forward to wash off her hands, he forced his attention back to his equipment, rapidly checking through it before tucking it away in the pack once more.

And she'd been right about the rain. The clouds were moving on, leaving them with a steady breeze that would probably have been more than a little chilly if not for the insulation of mud covering them.

"I don't think the gear is too far from here. Once we get there, I'll get a fire going for some water and you can wash up."

She looked up at him. "What about you?"

He needed a cold dousing in the middle of the river, but he didn't intend to tell her that. Once a woman knew she made you hot with a single look, she'd inevitably use it against you to her full advantage. "Afraid you're gonna have to be married to the Texas Mudman?"

"Better that than the British Madman," she countered as she stood.

She was still smiling, but Tyler knew instinctively that she was no longer amused. If anything, he thought she looked disconcerted, as if she didn't believe what she'd said.

He took her arm, helping her climb over a large boulder in their path. "Was he mad?"

"Most considered him to be a great statesman. He was the epitome of tall, powerful and charismatic." She stopped, looking back at him, the width of the hard stone between them. "Rather like you, actually.

Though he would have never tolerated any sort of mud bath.''

"And you? What did you consider him?"

Her lips twisted. "Once the bloom wore off, you mean?" She moved away from the rock, giving Tyler room to climb over. "Insane."

His eyes narrowed, not liking the implication. "I'm not insane, M."

"I don't care what you are," she replied flatly. "As long as we get into *la Fortuna*."

God help him, he had to remind himself that he didn't trust her. "Why is it so important to you?"

She tilted her head a little, as if measuring her words. "You want to help Westin because you owe him for saving your life," she eventually said. "I need to help him in order to get my life back." Then she turned on her very wet heel and headed down the riverbank.

Tyler watched her for a long while before following. Her hair, weighted with water and pale brown mud, nearly reached her waist, which seemed even narrower because of the way the soaked cotton pants and the water-heavy T-shirt clung to her lush curves.

He wasn't sure what distracted him more—her words or the view of her swaying hips.

What life was it that she wanted back? One that involved El Jefe, or one that didn't?

He wasn't sure he could wait much longer before knowing for certain.

Five

It was taking too long for the water to heat. And once it *was* hot, it would be nowhere enough to help Marisa feel clean again. The capacity of the pan from the mess kit Tyler had produced when they'd made it back to where he'd hidden the boat wasn't enough.

The fire was dancing, and the sun was rapidly heading down. If she were going to go in the river, the way Tyler had said he was doing before he'd disappeared a ways up the riverbank, she'd better do it while she could still see.

He'd left out another T-shirt for her to wear; he seemed to have a never-ending supply of the things. This one was dark blue and she carefully carried it, along with the pair of sweatpants he'd also left for her, over to a rock, being careful not to get any mud on either. Then she took the small cake of soap he'd left near the fire over to the water's edge.

A glance over her shoulder told her that Tyler was still nowhere in sight, and reminding herself of the number of times she'd bathed in the creek as a child before her parents let her go away for schooling in Belize, she peeled out of the filthy clothes and waded into the water.

It was colder than she'd expected, and the rocks beneath her bare feet were slippery, which meant that she didn't linger over the task. And after she finished washing out her hair using the hand soap, she feared that she *would* have to cut off her hair if only to get the tangles out of it.

The water was almost up to her shoulders and the current, though smooth, was swift. She hadn't realized she'd gone quite so far out into the river. The memory of white rapids was a little too close to the surface, and she swam toward the shore where she could stand a bit more steadily. She continued threading her fingers through her hair, trying to get the worst of the knots free. She looked up, caught by the vivid red and gold of the sunset. The colors shifted, deepened even as she watched. The goose pimples covering her arms and legs reminded her to pay attention, however, and she quickly rinsed her hair one last time, then rose from the water.

And then she saw him. Tyler.

Doing much the same thing as she, rising up from the water. He was far enough down the river that it was no wonder she hadn't seen him before he stood.

Transfixed, she could do nothing but stare. He was…beautiful. Despite the distance, she could see the sinew roping his shoulders, the muscles defining his powerful legs. As she watched in that last light of day, he crossed one arm across his rib cage and leaned back one more time in the water, seeming to float for a moment, before he submerged himself, and came out with one sharp flick of his head that sent water flying from him in a sharp arch of diamond glitter.

She didn't even like the man! Yet there she was, staring at him like some silly, smitten teenager over a movie star.

Disgusted with herself, she hurried out of the water, drying off furiously fast before yanking the shirt over her bare skin. The last thing she wanted was for him to make it back to their little camp and find her still floundering around in the water, too distracted by the sight of him to do anything but breathe. Still moving rapidly, she used the soap to wash out her bra and panties. They'd once been pristine ivory, but now were tinted a permanent coffee color, courtesy of the mud that had stained every inch of fabric she'd been wearing.

Tyler may seem to possess an endless supply of T-shirts, but he didn't come equipped with women's lingerie, so, discolored or not, they'd have to do. She draped them over a branch, and went back to stoke the fire. Now that she was out of the cold river, the evening felt temperate and she tossed the sweatpants under the shelter. She'd save them for later when the night grew colder.

She had no way of knowing if Tyler would be one minute longer, or ten. Calling upon skills she'd long ago left behind, she rummaged through some of his supplies, then went to the river's edge and tossed out the line. While she was waiting on that, she found several suitable branches and whittled off the ends with one of his knives.

By the time Tyler did return, she wished she'd had a camera to capture the priceless look on his face. Stunned didn't come close to it as he eyed the two fish sizzling on the spit over the fire. The pleasure of that was even greater than knowing she hadn't forgotten everything that she'd once learned at her mother's knees, and it went a long way toward helping her not think about the way he'd looked, rising like some Neptune god from the diamond-bright river.

He walked over to the fire and seemed to study the setup. It wasn't quite as perfect as what he'd done the day before—it *had* been a long time since she'd been at her mother's knee, after all—but Marisa was nevertheless pleased with her efforts.

But all he said was, "You've been in my stuff."

The world screeched to a halt as her pleasure whooshed out of her as abruptly as a pinpricked balloon. Since it was obvious that she had, indeed, been in "his stuff," she declined to comment. She turned the fish one last time, then pulled the skewers away from the flame and propped them to cool against the circle of rocks around the fire.

She waited for him to say something more, to castigate her, to put her in her place. He did none of those things. After a moment, she nudged the fragrant trout onto the plate from his mess kit, broke the skewer in half and dropped the slender pieces of wood into the flame. Then she took the other fish, and sat, a little away from the heat of the fire, tucking her T-shirt and her legs carefully beneath her.

She was aware of him watching her as she gingerly picked the hot fish right off the skewer with her fingers and ate. He spread out his cammies on a stumpy palm far away from the one where she'd hung her underwear, as if he didn't want even his wet clothes to come within touching distance of her things. She felt like a fool for being hurt.

What she should have been was relieved that he didn't make some stupid, lewd comment about her bra and panties.

The small black duffel that went everywhere with him—including bath time, apparently—he zipped up inside a larger one. He went to the boat and fiddled with the outboard, before turning toward the fire.

Something went tight and uncomfortable inside her stomach.

She'd left a small pile of figs piled on the rocks and he picked one up as he sat down on the ground across the circle of the fire from her and cut it into quarters with his pocketknife.

He didn't touch the fish.

"What's the matter, Murdoch?" she finally asked. "Afraid I drugged your fish?"

He didn't answer and disbelief swept through her. She'd been speaking facetiously! "Eat that, then." She flung her skewer and the partially eaten fish at him.

He smoothly caught the skewer before it could bean him on the head, and set it on the rocks. With barely a hitch in his movements, he continued eating the fig.

"Why aren't you afraid to eat the fruit?" Her voice rose and she struggled to contain it. "Maybe it's tainted, too."

"With what?"

She was practically vibrating with fury as she stood. "Whatever my evil self put into your fish!"

"Calm down."

"I won't!"

As if he hadn't just accused her of God knew what, he held up a slice of fig between his knife and thumb in offering.

She recoiled. "You are odious."

He shrugged and ate the last quarter of the fruit. "Suit yourself."

"What on earth would I have to gain by hurting you?"

"Maybe nothing," he drawled agreeably. "Maybe everything. Why don't you tell me?"

"I wouldn't tell you the time of day, even if I still had my watch." She wanted to storm off in an annoyed huff. But where was there to storm to? It was far too early to lie down in the shelter; she'd never go to sleep as wound up as she was.

So she paced. She had to do something with the energy bubbling in her veins. But as she rounded the close confines of their small camp, passing by the boat that he'd dragged well up the shore, her anger increased. "What were you doing with the motor a little while ago, anyway? Putting back some little piece that you'd removed to disable it while you washed in the river?"

"Yes."

She blinked, unable to believe that she could be even more stung by his actions. Yet she was. "Well, fine." She turned on her heel, ready to go to the shelter, no matter how early it was, no matter how wound up she was, because being in his presence was absolutely more than she could stand.

The immovable tree root that caught her toe, however, had other things in mind. She pitched forward, yelping as she caught herself from falling, snatching up her foot to rub the toe that felt as if it had been shoved straight back toward her heel.

Tyler was beside her before she was even aware of him moving. ''Were you bit? What?''

She jerked her shoulder away from him and hobbled over to sit by the fire. ''I stubbed my toe,'' she muttered. She got just what she deserved for stomping around barefoot in the dark like an ill-tempered child.

He crouched down at her feet. ''Let me see.''

She tried to draw her leg back, but he'd wrapped his long fingers around her ankle and all of her bottled tension suddenly focused its considerable force on the feel of his touch.

She was glad it was as dark as it was, that the fire had simmered down to little more than a red glow.

''This one?''

She nearly jerked out of her skin when he smoothed his thumb over her big toe. It infuriated her, absolutely infuriated her, that her libido would decide—with this man who was ten parts obnoxious and one miserly little part *not*—to reawaken after being so dormant that she'd wondered if she'd ever feel an interest in a man again.

''Well?'' He was waiting.

''Yes, that one,'' she agreed hurriedly. ''It's fine. Really. Just a stub.''

But he merely lifted her foot closer to the glow of the fire, so he could see better, she presumed, as she hurriedly grabbed the hem of the T-shirt and held it down against her thighs where it belonged.

"At least it's not bleeding."

"Um, no." She pulled back again, to no avail. "Tyler, really—"

"You've got blisters on your heels."

How she could have forgotten, she didn't know. "I know. My shoes—"

"Why didn't you say so?"

"And what?" She dragged the T-shirt hem an inch closer to her knees. If she could have, she'd have pulled it right down to her ankles. "You'd have stopped? Let me wait on the side of the mountain until you'd done your thing up at the top? I doubt it. You couldn't even go bathe in the river without making certain I couldn't do something to foil your plans."

"We could have put some stuff on your heels to keep them from getting this bad."

His utterly reasonable tone set her teeth on edge just as much as his refusal to deny his distrust of her. When he went to one of his precious bags and came back with some type of ointment and adhesive pads, she snatched them from him. "*I* will do it."

"Knock yourself out."

It wasn't easy. She had to keep the hem of the

T-shirt pulled down to a reasonably modest length, while still being able to reach her heels. After she'd dropped one of the adhesives in the dirt, Tyler muttered under his breath and pried the bandages out of her fingers.

"We don't have enough to waste," he said flatly. "Give me your foot."

"No!"

He looked a little less than patient. "For God's sake, M., does everything have to be a battle with you?"

"You are the one who drew the battle lines. From the minute we met, you've been horrible to me. Why would I want your help any more than you've made it abundantly clear you don't want mine?"

"You needed my help plenty when I was breathing air into you and pumping water out of your lungs."

"I—" She broke off. He'd given her CPR? She had no way to be certain he wasn't manipulating her even now, with his words. But the truth was, she didn't know what all he'd done when he'd pulled her out of the river. All she remembered was thinking she was going to die there in the river, so close to her family, but as far away as ever.

And then she'd been lying on the bank with him leaning over her.

"You might just as well have left me there to

drown," she said thickly, "despite my future use-fulness."

"Shut up and give me your feet. We'll be lucky if those heels don't get infected at this rate. You should have said something sooner."

He reached for her feet and she inched away. "And have you accuse me of deliberately slowing us up? No thanks."

"What do you think is going to happen if you get an infection?" Again, he reached and she backed away. Even in the faint light she could see the way his face hardened. "Marisa, I am seriously getting pissed off here. Give me your damned feet."

"Well, if you're going to be angry, then so be it. I'm angry, too." Not caring whether she displayed a complete lack of dignity or not, she scrambled away from him and stood, yanking the T-shirt well down her thighs. "You can't accuse me of being in league with El Jefe one minute, insult me, and then turn around being all...all *nice,*" she spat the word, "the next minute."

"When did I insult you?"

"You wouldn't even touch the fish!"

"I don't like fish, all right?" He shoved his fingers through his hair, making the short, thick strands stand on end. "It'll keep us from starving, but if I don't have to eat the stuff, I'm not going to."

"Then you could have just said that! Instead of implying that I'd done something to it."

"You're the one who suggested it."

"I was being facetious! I didn't think you really thought that, until you just sat there, stone-faced." Her shoulders drooped and she lifted her hands slightly. "I don't understand why you can't trust in me, Tyler. I just don't get it. All I want is to get this mission over with."

"So you can get your life back."

"Yes."

"You're hiding something."

"I am not!" She turned her back on her niggling conscience. Franco had nothing to do with his mission. Nothing at all.

His lips twisted. "I can see it in your face, M. In your eyes. You're hiding something, and until I know what it is..." He left the rest hanging.

"Then I'll remain outside of the cozy twosome of people you do trust," she finished.

"It's better that way."

"For whom?" she asked bitterly. "Only you, Murdoch. Only you."

"For us both."

"That's ridiculous. Why is it better for me to be someone you'd dismantle a motor over!"

"Because I want you," he said flatly. "And I don't want to want you."

The words seemed to hang there in the night. Marisa swayed slightly. He couldn't have said that. Could he?

"Not trusting you at least keeps you at a distance." He grimaced. "And don't pretend that you're unaware of it."

He most certainly had said it. "I don't—"

"I saw you in the river, too, M. I saw you watching me."

Her lips parted. And though the dark, verdant forest was rich with oxygen, she suddenly felt unable to breathe. He lifted his hand and seemed to wince a little when she flinched. But he continued the movement and touched her chin.

She shivered at the grazing touch.

"Even before then," he said, "I wanted you. Even covered in mud. It didn't matter. You know what it does to a man to want a woman he can't afford to trust?"

She swallowed, tried to moisten her dry lips. Just then she couldn't be any less than honest, no matter how much it revealed. "Perhaps the same thing it does to a woman who wants a man after she's vowed never to trust another."

His jaw cocked. His eyes were hooded, unreadable in the night. His thumb smoothed over the point of her chin and brushed back up to tease the very corner of her lips.

She stopped breathing altogether.

"Helluva note, isn't it?" he finally said. He dropped his hand and moved away.

Marisa felt as if the temperature had suddenly dropped ten degrees.

It was just the wind, she told herself. It often picked up at night. He hadn't been going to kiss her. It was a ludicrous thought. "I wouldn't have done anything to the boat," she said after a moment. "Though I don't expect you'll believe that."

He sat down by the fire and poked the glowing embers with a stick, causing a small fountain of sparks to spurt up from the wood. "Don't expect anything, Marisa, and life is easier all the way around."

Why did those words sound so unbearably lonely? He was only referring to their situation. Wasn't he?

"My *abuela* used to say that people rise to your expectations," she said after a taut moment. "She also said that people sink to them just as easily."

"Is there a point in there?"

She knew he was only baiting her. And it almost worked. She waited a moment to let the irritation settle. "I guess it's only that if you expect nothing, then nothing is just what you'll get." Which was a sad thing, as far as she was concerned. She stifled a sigh and headed toward the shelter. "Good night, Murdoch."

Neither one of them thought about the blisters on her heels. Not until hours later when it began to rain again.

Hard, driving rain.

Cold, stinging, miserable rain.

At the first hiss of raindrops hitting the remains of the fire, he'd flipped over the boat atop their clothes and gear to keep them dry. He'd huddled in a rain poncho, feeling that godawful ache in his chest from ribs that had taken one beating too many in the past few days, knowing that Marisa was under the shelter as dry as you please, for about as long as he'd been able to stand it.

"You're getting soft in your old age, Murdoch," he muttered to himself when he finally gave up and headed toward the shelter. He flipped off the rain poncho and ducked into the shelter, prepared for an argument from Marisa, because he wasn't entirely certain that she was sleeping. She'd been silent for hours, but that didn't necessarily prove much.

Several staccato cracks of lightning lit the shadows under the sharply pitched tarp and he could see that Marisa was stretched out on her stomach, her profusion of curls streaming around her shoulders. And below the ruched up bottom of the sweatpants she'd finally put on, her bare heels stared up at him accusingly.

It wasn't like him to forget anything, but he'd clean forgotten about her heels.

He went back into the driving rain, guided only by the intermittent flashes of lightning and felt around the increasingly muddy ground for the tube of ointment. The bandages would be useless at this point after laying in the rain. There were only a few left in the first-aid kit, so they'd have to use them in the morning when she'd have to put her shoes back on to continue the trek.

He found the tube quickly enough, though he was soaked through by the time he did. Wondering just how wet it would be if it *were* the rainy season, he used the water still in the pan to wash the mud from his hands, then stripped out of the sopping shirt and tossed it onto the bush. The only blessing was that the slanted rain was not headed right through the open side of the shelter, leaving that space relatively untouched.

He silently slid in beside Marisa and carefully tucked her outflung arm back beside her to give himself some room. She didn't stir, and he was glad for it. He didn't know what stupidity had taken hold of his mouth earlier to admit what he had. If he was lucky, the rain would ease up and he'd be out of the shelter again well before dawn and she'd never know he'd invaded her space this way.

Sitting forward without either taking out one of

the supports holding up the shelter or dripping water all over her was no easy task, but he managed, as he carefully slathered the broken, blistered skin on her heels with the first aid ointment.

She made a soft sound. Not a moan. Not a sigh. But somewhere in between, and it felt as though that half-husky sound shot straight into his bloodstream.

Tyler very nearly slid right back out into the driving rain. It was damn inconvenient the way his body had a mind of its own. If it were any other time, any other situation, he'd have pursued Marisa until they both got what they wanted. And then he'd have walked away, knowing neither one of them had expectations of anything more.

But it wasn't any other time.

As Tyler stretched out on his back and stared into the inky void that was alleviated only by the harsh flashes of lightning, he reminded himself that a man's life hung in the balance while he was merely being inconvenienced by an untimely case of the hots for his so-called traveling companion.

Unfortunately the perspective didn't do a damn thing to keep him from hearing the soft sound of her breath, from feeling the dry, cozy warmth of her curvaceous body scant inches away from his rain-soaked one, from smelling the scent of his soap on her body and in her hair.

So Tyler lay there.

Counting the strikes of lightning until the minutes between them began to lengthen, and the storm slowly rolled onward.

And even then, Tyler lay there.

Wanting the woman beside him. Knowing he could never reach for her.

Not even if he *did* trust her.

Six

"What on earth do you think you're doing?" The husky, soft voice was next to Tyler's ear, not at all matching the sentiment behind the words.

Beyond the confines of their shelter, nature all around them was alive and kicking. Birds were calling, monkeys were screeching. It felt, just then, as if he and the woman in his arms were the only two people on earth. Marisa's almond-shaped eyes were barely open. Soft with sleep, they were...bewitching, dammit. And he was hard as a rock.

He stretched, groaning. "I'm gettin' too old for this," he muttered. He was stiff everywhere, most particularly against the softness of the woman sprawled across his chest. His hands just sort of naturally wanted to head back down to rest on the small of her back. Right where his fingertips could explore the sweep of her hips, the curve of her rear. His teeth ground together and he redirected his hands safely to her shoulders.

Shoulders that he gently lifted and pushed off him.

"What am I doing?" His lips twisted at the irony. "Getting up."

The rain had stopped, thankfully. And the morning was full of pale, silvery light. Even though he knew the danger of it, he couldn't help but look at Marisa and wonder whether her eyes would get more golden or more brown when she was being well and thoroughly loved. In a minute, he knew that drowsiness in them would clear and she'd probably scramble away from him like he was the odious thing she believed him to be.

But right now she looked warm and soft and way too appealing with her body draped in *his* T-shirt.

Which meant he definitely needed to get away from her. Right now. "Make sure you get the bandages on your heels today. We'll be hoofing it from here on out."

He ducked from the shelter, and Marisa rubbed her eyes, watching him go. He'd obviously slept in the shelter with her. Yet she hadn't awakened when he'd snuck in.

Somehow, that bothered her. No, that wasn't quite right. It bothered her because it *didn't* bother her that she'd slept through him joining her under the tarp where there was little extra space after one person, much less a man of his size.

And despite the expected bit of ache from sleeping on the ground instead of a mattress, Marisa realized that she'd slept well. Surprisingly well.

It confused her, and Marisa didn't much like being confused.

Sighing, she sat up and examined her heels. They were sore, even without touching them. She also realized they'd been covered with the ointment that she knew she'd never gotten around to using.

Which meant that Tyler had done it. Another thing that she'd slept right through.

"You're mine." Gerald's handsome face was red with fury when she'd refused, yet again, to get that ridiculous tattoo of his name put on her body. It had started out as a joke. Or so she'd thought. Until one morning, after he'd actually brought a person to their home to do the job and she'd had to lock herself in her room to make her refusal clear. The locked door that had seemed to protect her from the tattoo artist had not protected her from Gerald, though. He'd picked the lock while she'd slept and she'd awakened, panicked, when he'd been sliding up her nightgown. He'd been holding a red pen in his hand. And while he held her down, he'd written his name, messily because of her struggling, across her hip.

Marisa shook her head, clearing it of the memory. She didn't want to think about what had happened after that.

So she started to crawl out of the shelter, stopping only when her hand landed on a soft piece of something. Her bra and panties. Obviously Tyler's doing, as well.

She bundled them up in her hand and crawled out of the shelter and stood. Near the trees, Tyler had spread out his gear and seemed to be repacking it. He wore those cammies and hiking boots again, and a tan shirt hung loose from his broad shoulders. He looked over his shoulder at her once, then turned back to what he was doing.

Everything was wet though it wasn't raining now, and she knew then what had spurred him to take shelter under the tarp. It had had nothing to do with her at all, and everything to do with sitting out all night in the rain.

It should have comforted her to know that.

He'd left one of his shirts on the ground right by the shelter. Obviously it was meant to wipe her feet, because it already bore the evidence that he'd done the same. She did so, then slid her toes into her shoes that had also been placed, conveniently, right there. There was no way she could fully put the shoes on, yet. Her heels were simply too raw. And they'd have been worse if not for him putting on the ointment while she'd slept.

She didn't want to think that it was thoughtfulness that had prompted Tyler's actions. It was far more likely simple expedience, she told herself as she headed down the riverbank for some privacy.

The dawn light was strengthening when she returned. He was obviously in the process of condensing his gear down to the small pack he'd used the previous day, and one other, larger one. For a moment she wondered where he'd gotten it, but then realized it was one of the bags he'd already had, the straps cleverly repositioned.

The shelter was gone. Something else was missing as well, she realized. "Where's the boat?"

He kept right on buttoning up his shirt. "Gone."

"Well, thank you. I noticed that." She gave him back the plastic holder containing the hand soap that she'd taken with her. "Gone where? And why?"

"We don't need it anymore."

It was no more information than she'd expected him to impart. She supposed he'd probably deflated it and done something clever with the little outboard to keep it from ever being found or used again.

She'd wet down her hair again at the river in an attempt to tame it, and now she tugged and pulled it into a braid that she tied off with a narrow strip she'd made by tearing out the sleeves of the T-shirt. She'd used the other sleeve as a sort of washcloth, and all things considered—sweatpants several sizes too large, and a T-shirt with no sleeves—she felt at least presentable.

She still had not covered her heels with the adhesive bandages, and he'd left several sitting out, along with the tube of antibiotic ointment and another pair of socks. So, while Tyler was absorbed in whatever it was he was holding, she perched on a rock and dealt with her heels. The shoes were a tight fit when she put them on, but they were just going to have to do. It wasn't as if she had an alternative, after all. Then she used the insect repellent and the sunblock that he'd left out, as well.

Her stomach rumbled, loud enough for Tyler to hear. She was too practical to be terribly embarrassed, though, when he just tossed her one of his protein bars and indicated the banana beside him that she hadn't noticed.

She practically fell on the fruit, so happy was she to see it. "Where'd you find them?" she asked after she'd peeled it and consumed nearly half of it. It was far too ripe, but she didn't care. To her, it was practically heaven.

"I wrestled a monkey for it."

"Right." She rolled her eyes and finished it off, then eyed the gadget in his hands with curiosity. "You brought a pager all the way out here? What on earth for?"

Tyler let his palm go flat, and the small square thing sat in plain sight. "It's not a pager," he said. "It's a GPS system." He watched Marisa's expression and felt something inside him go cold at the gleam that entered her eyes. And he'd thought he was as cold inside as a man could get.

"I've seen them," she said. "One of my regulars at the restaurant has one he takes camping. Only his was larger. More like a television remote."

"It'll get the job done." His assurance was flat, but it didn't seem to dim her excitement.

"Can you use it to get us rescued?"

"I told you already. *We* don't need rescuing. Westin does."

Her smooth forehead crinkled. "You've said that before. But if we got help, then we could get to him more quickly. And time is critical, is it not?"

"Using this thing before I need to could end up bringing El Jefe right to our doorstep." If they weren't already. He watched Marisa, and wondered what she'd do now. It had been a calculated risk, bringing the receiver right out into the open. He said nothing about the fact that it was also a transmitter; that it was going to get his and Westin's butts out of *la Fortuna* when he needed it. "That's why I didn't use it to determine our location."

She had brains. She'd probably figure out the rest on her own. And if she was going to prove herself, one way or the other, he figured today was as good a day as any. Because with each passing hour, the more certain he was that El Jefe was on to them.

First Westin had been captured—an unusual thing in itself. Then Luke had been injured trying to get to Westin using, as it turned out, his own clandestine resources. Now Tyler's own efforts had been seriously curtailed.

There just weren't that many coincidences in the world as far as Tyler was concerned. And if Marisa really was part of the enemy, he wanted her to make her move before he got anywhere near *la Fortuna*.

"Well, we certainly don't want El Jefe's thugs to come calling." As if she'd lost any interest in the device on his palm, she balled up the banana peel and tossed it aside. Then she looked up at him, and went oddly still.

Tyler started to tuck the deactivated device in his pocket. When Marisa moved suddenly, snatching up the machete that was near his feet, he froze.

This was it, then.

He'd wanted her to make a move, and she was. Only it wasn't toward the GPS device, after all. His muscles flexed as he prepared for her to move. He knew he could stop her, and felt a fleeting guilt because, when it came down to it, he really didn't want to hurt her.

Then she moved. He pivoted. And the broad blade of the heavy knife passed right by his face in a blur of motion before stabbing into the tree bare inches behind him.

He barely had time to utter an oath when Marisa shuddered, backing away from him. He turned to see a vividly patterned snake, not dead but writhing madly against the tree where the machete had very effectively pinned it. Marisa turned away, looking as if she wanted to retch.

And Tyler knew a moment's unease that maybe, just maybe, he was wrong about her.

He finished the job she'd begun and the fer-de-lance fell, harmless, into the tangled ground cover where it would end up food for some other creature.

Marisa was still shuddering. "I knew someone who died from one of those," she finally whispered. "He was only nine. I've hated the forest ever since." She tossed her thick, long braid behind her back and visibly shook off the memory. "Am I supposed to carry one of those?" She pointed at the packs.

He also didn't want to admire her practicality. But there was something about the way she focused on the matter at hand that got to him.

He handed her the daypack, and hefted the larger one on his back. She lifted the daypack experimentally as if testing its weight, then tucked the uneaten protein bar and the tubes of ointment, sunblock and repellent inside before slipping her arms through the straps. "What about the rest of our stuff?"

"Nonessential."

"Sort of like my suitcase," she said, her voice smooth.

"Sort of." He wiped the single smear from the machete and sheathed it.

If Marisa were going to make a move against him, she hadn't done it yet. Hell, she could have just let the lethal snake do its thing if it really had been intending to strike him.

He pitched the "non-essentials" into the river and watched until everything disappeared—sank or floated away on the current. Then grabbing a heavy palm, he wiped away their footprints and all other traces of their presence as they headed away from their camp.

"You are so totally paranoid, Murdoch," she murmured as he tossed the palm into the river when they'd left the sandy, muddy bank for the stretch of river rock that they'd follow for now.

"Just 'cause you're paranoid doesn't mean they're not out to get you," he said blandly.

She snorted softly. And they set off, picking their way carefully over the jagged, shifting rocks.

"You were pretty handy with that machete," he eventually said. He could hear her shoes on the rocks behind him. They'd be lucky if she didn't break an ankle because of the smooth soles.

"Is that your version of a thank-you?" Her voice was a little breathless.

His lips twisted. "Take it how you want, M."

"Un idiot entêté."

Idiot. It wasn't hard to grasp the sentiment behind the words. And he was glad she was behind him. Because, for some reason, her huffy utterance made him grin.

"Murdoch's window was three weeks."

Ricky Mercado nodded. He didn't look at the British officer who'd spoken to him. Just because Tyler hadn't made it to the field near the Mezcayan border to exchange the plane for the Jeep didn't mean the mission was scrapped. "We picked up Ms. Rodriguez's ID and credentials at the airfield just as scheduled." So things had been on target then, at least. "He'll do it in three weeks," he said flatly. Knowing Ty, it might even be less.

Unless he was dead.

"We captured another group of men crossing the border yesterday. They were terrorizing a caravan of students traveling from Belize City to Mexico. El Jefe's moves into Belize from Mezcaya won't be tolerated."

Again, Ricky nodded. "Yes, sir, I heard. But your government agreed to support this mission with the United States. Tyler will get Westin out and then you can get on with your efforts to eradicate El Jefe. Everyone wants them stopped." Everyone, including

Lieutenant Colonel Westin, who'd been detailed by the United States government to work with the British base located in Belize to stomp out El Jefe's reign of terror from spreading into that country. Everyone had a vested interest in putting El Jefe out of commission.

"You don't even know whether Murdoch and his companion are still alive. There has been no sign of them since we discovered what was left of his plane. The wreckage clearly indicated it exploded on impact."

"Three weeks," Ricky reminded, turning around to eye the other officer. No matter what had happened in the past, he refused to believe that Tyler had gone down that way. He couldn't believe it. "If you send in troops to El Jefe's compound before then, Westin will most certainly die. And I can guarantee you, sir, that the international incident everyone is hoping to avoid will explode in our faces."

The officer's eyes cooled. "Are you threatening me?"

Ricky didn't much care what the other man thought. He turned and looked out the window once more. "Three weeks," was all he said.

"It's a bridge."

"It's a flippin' Mayan artifact."

Marisa propped her hand wearily on her hip and

glared at Tyler. The sun was high in the sky: it was hot and almost unbearably humid. Even without her watch, she knew they'd been hiking for hours. Over the past few days, she'd gotten so she could judge time passed in accordance with the ache in her feet.

"Murdoch, if we cross here, we'll cut off miles. We can go over the mountain instead of all the way around it!"

"If we cross here, we'll end up down there." His hooded gaze was directed down the deep chasm. They'd long ago left the river behind and had been following this particular ridge for some time. He'd been hoping to find a likely crossing point as it was simply too steep and rough to descend otherwise.

"No, we won't. All the bridges around here are like this," she assured. "They're stronger than they look."

"No." He pulled the binoculars from his pack. It didn't matter that she was right about the shortcut. They did need to get across the chasm. And the sooner, the better, he thought silently as he watched a tiny moving point far off in the distance. It was definitely a person. He could easily make out the pale hair—or maybe a light-colored hat—against the plethora of green surrounding him. He also could see the telltale glint of the sun reflecting off a rifle. The guy was steadily gaining on them. "We'll find another crossing point further—"

He lowered the binoculars and turned to Marisa only to find her already starting across the narrow bridge. "Dammit! Marisa, come back here now."

"Thought you were a big, strong military man," she called back as she gingerly stepped from one board to the next, hands curled over the fraying rope that was supposed to pass for handrails.

He stuffed the binoculars in his pack and started after her. "Talk about an imbecile," he grumbled, as the bridge shifted and groaned the moment he set foot on it. "Marisa!"

She was nearly halfway across. "Tyler, you know I'm—" She screamed when the rotting board beneath her foot gave way and her leg went through right past her knee.

Chills streaked down his spine. In an instant, he went down on his knees, distributing his weight. "I know you're a damn walking accident," he said through gritted teeth as he cautiously slid his knee across one plank to the next. "Just hang on."

"No kidding," she gasped. She had one arm wrapped around a board, and the other twined in the rope support. "The other board is cracking, too."

"Then don't put any weight on it."

It was an achingly slow process, creeping out over what he considered to be a death trap. He still had yards to go to reach her, but he could see her white face. The way she kept looking down. He needed to distract her. "Did I ever tell you about the day my golfing buddies and I found a baby on the golf course?"

She closed her eyes and when she opened them, she was looking at him. "You know you didn't. You're just making it up to be outrageous." Her voice was little more than a whisper.

He slid past another plank. "Well, okay, I know I didn't tell you already. But it's true. There she was in her carrier on the ninth tee of the Lone Star Country Club, all tucked up snug as a bug with a note pinned to her blanket."

"Who would do such a thing?"

"Nobody's figured that out just yet." He crossed another plank. And another. The bridge rocked, groaned. He kept his voice easy, his tone casual, and as a distraction, telling her about the odd occurrence last year was fitting the bill. But when they got off this thing, he was going to strangle her. "My friend Flynt and his wife are taking care of the baby until we figure out who her daddy is."

"Lucky b-baby. Some places would have stuck her in foster care." She closed her eyes, and he could see her visibly control her trembling. "I can't see you playing golf."

"Too civilized for the likes of me?"

She managed a shaky smile, but her eyes were terrified. "Yes."

"Just hold on, Marisa, I'm almost there. You're just fine. You haven't slipped any more. You're more on the bridge than off. Okay? You ever been to a circus?"

She nodded, her eyes glued to his. "Is it too late to say you were right?" she asked shakily.

"Definitely." He slid up beside her. "Way too late. This is what we're gonna do. I'm gonna take your wrists, and you're gonna hold on to mine exactly the same way. Just like the trapeze artists at the circus. Our arms'll be linked. Then I'll pull you up. Got it?" He slowly wrapped his hands around her wrists.

He could see her swallow, and knew she was thinking about that brief moment when she'd have to let go in order to grab him. "I'm not going to let you fall," he said.

Her eyes searched his. "Even though you don't trust me."

He tightened his grip. For a taller than average, curvy woman, right then she felt painfully delicate. "Even though. Come on, Marisa. Grab my wrists before we both end up down there."

That seemed enough to prompt her. As if in slow motion, he saw her eyes close. Her lips moved silently. After a moment, she moved. First one, then the other more quickly, she wrapped her hands, tight and strong, around his wrists, completing the link between them.

He allowed himself a long breath as he adjusted to her weight. "Good girl," he murmured.

She smiled weakly.

Then he was pulling her free of the rotting board, and she clung to him, there on that narrow, swaying excuse of a bridge, high above the rest of the world. "I'm sorry." Her voice was fervent.

He shrugged off the idiotic notion that he could hold her like that for about a month of Sundays, and carefully moved her hands to the ropes again. "Don't stand up," he said flatly. "We've still got to get to the other side. We're already halfway across the damn thing, so we might as well go the rest." It couldn't be any more dangerous than returning the way they'd come.

But two more boards split apart and fell, silently, swiftly, toward the base of the chasm before they made it. When they got to the other side, he yanked Marisa well away from the edge, feeling adrenaline surging through his system like newly struck oil. "You're crazy, you know that?"

"Tyler, I'm sorry, I—"

"Shut up. Just shut the hell up." He shoved his hands through her hair and covered her mouth with his.

Marisa stiffened like a board, her fingers going to

his wrists once more, intent on pushing him away. But his lips were warm and surprisingly soft, and without conscious thought, instead of pushing away, she held on.

Back and forth his lips gently, tantalizingly, irresistibly brushed over hers. She murmured his name and nearly moaned when his tongue slipped along her inner lip.

And her mind simply went blank.

All she could do then was feel. And taste. And think, in the very back of her fogged brain, that never in her life had she been kissed quite like his.

When he finally lifted his head, she swayed weakly, twining her fingers into the coarse fabric of his shirt for support. ''You...'' She swallowed, pressed her forehead against his chest and moistened her lips. ''You shouldn't have done that.''

His wide chest moved in a deep breath. ''Probably not,'' he agreed roughly.

And then he tipped back her head and kissed her again. One arm went around her, his large palm splayed against the small of her back, urging her against him. And she, oh she couldn't ever remember feeling quite so alive. Quite so perfectly feminine as he fitted her curves against him, letting her know undeniably that they were indeed very much alive.

And he was just as aroused as she.

Her daypack hit the ground with a thud and a puff of dust. His hands slid under the back of her shirt, fingertips gliding along her spine.

Her knees went to water, and he caught her about the waist. Mindless, she arched against him, exhaling deeply when he tugged the shirt from her altogether and pressed his lips to her throat. Her fingers sank into his hair and she stared blindly into the endless blue above them. Her heartbeat felt slow and heavy even as it raced in her chest, until she felt dizzy with it.

His kiss burned over her shoulder, up her neck, finally finding her seeking mouth yet again, and she cried out when his hard, warm hand finally glided along the narrow strap of her bra and slowly, oh, so slowly drew the stretchy fabric away from the aching tip.

He lifted his head, and she swallowed hard as his dark eyes surveyed his handiwork. His jaw was tight, his lips pressed together. Only the heat burning in the depths of his eyes told her that he was far from being put off by her abundant breasts. Then he drew his finger along the edge of satin and she thought she may well collapse when he urged the other cup aside.

Her nipples tightened even more under his steady gaze. Her lips parted for air, her fingers tangling in the buttons of his shirt. She was desperate to feel his bare skin. To feel his chest against hers. To have nothing at all between them.

But when she yanked apart the buttons, popping one right off in her haste, and she spread the lapels of his shirt, it wasn't an expanse of muscle and sinew that she saw. It was an expanse of blue and green and yellow, visible through his dusting of chest hair; one of the most vicious bruises she'd ever seen in her lifetime.

She scrambled back from him, utterly and completely horrified as she yanked her bra into place before tugging his shirt away even more fully. "You're hurt!"

Tyler made a rough sound. He tried to slide his arms around her waist again, but she wriggled away. "Marisa—"

"Why didn't you say something?"

Her touch was light as a feather as she felt along his bruised rib cage, but it still made his nerves nearly explode. Not from pain, but because he wanted her hands *all* over him. And he was a damn fool for letting things get this out of hand.

"Please don't tell me that you've had a broken rib all this time." She was sliding under his arm, going behind him, tugging at the backpack that he'd all but forgotten because he'd been more concerned with exploring every inch of the infernal woman's body.

"It's not broken," he assured. "Just bruised, and it's healing. Come back here."

Again, she evaded him. "How did it happen? When the plane went down? It takes a while for a bruise to color that much, doesn't it?"

"I don't know what hit me when we went down."

"How do you know it's not broken?"

"Because I've had broken ribs before. Trust me, it's a bruise." He tugged her back into his arms and caught her earlobe gently between his teeth. "Just a bruise," he said again.

She shivered against him, her knees weak. "Tyler, we shouldn't—"

"I know." He did know it. They shouldn't. For about a dozen reasons, not the least of which, he was technically on duty. She might be part of El Jefe, in which case, he'd deserve the knife she'd stick in his back if only because of his own stupidity. If she wasn't part of El Jefe, and really was on the mission because of the vague reasons she'd admitted, then he had no business whatsoever not protecting her to his fullest ability.

Which also meant protecting her from *him* as well as any others. "I know," he said again. He took a long breath, soaking up the feel of her satiny, rich skin against him, then stepped back from her. He handed her the shirt that he dimly remembered tearing over her head, and then the small pack.

"Oh, no," she said, as she held it up by the straps. "Not so fast." And damn if the woman didn't go to his pack and begin flipping free the straps to pull stuff from inside.

"What on God's green earth do you think you're doing?" He crouched down beside her, yanking the bundles of clothes and supplies out of her hands. "We're too exposed to camp here, and we've got hours of daylight left."

"I'm not stupid," she countered. "I know that. But my pack is less than half full. There's no reason for you to carry all the weight."

He was surprised enough for a minute that she actually managed to stuff some of the gear into her own daypack before he stopped her. Even Sonya, who'd been an equal member of his team before she'd been exposed as the traitor she was, had never concerned herself with lightening someone else's load.

Then Marisa held up the fat pack of gum that he'd carefully tucked in the middle of his pack. "Been holding out on me, Murdoch?"

He grabbed the packet and stuffed it back into his belongings. "Yeah," he said flatly. "That's enough, now. There wasn't enough weight in there to start with to bother me."

She blinked at his brusqueness, but it couldn't be

helped. He let her take some of the clothing, since it seemed particularly important to her.

Silent, as if nothing had just transpired between them at all, she slid her arms through the straps of the pack and flipped her braid free. "I still don't get you, Murdoch," she finally said as she struck out in front of him, heading into the sun.

He watched her backside, distinctly uncomfortable at the feelings inside him. Sex was easy enough to get beyond. He'd done it before. He'd do it again. He was a soldier. He was used to putting everything aside for the sake of the battle. And there were no two ways about it. It was a battle against El Jefe that he and the rest of the decent world were waging.

So what was it, then, about Marisa that sneaked under his skin, making it damn impossible to ignore?

Right then, he didn't "get" himself, any more than Marisa did.

Seven

It *was* a blond-haired man following them, Tyler decided.

Three days had passed since the bridge, and the man tracking them had made no moves to lessen the distance.

On the fourth day, however, he did.

Tyler had determined the man was traveling alone, and was capable of making better time than he and Marisa were. He'd also figured it was only a matter of time before the guy made his move. Maybe he'd been waiting for Tyler and Marisa to be lulled into a false sense of security by the continual distance he'd been maintaining. Maybe he'd wanted to bide his time to see just where Tyler and Marisa were heading. Maybe he'd been waiting for Marisa to make some move.

Even though his companion seemed completely ignorant of the guy tracking them, and had made no moves whatsoever on the GPS, Tyler made himself consider that last possibility.

Regardless of their tracker's reasoning, though, on

that particular day, the guy started moving faster. And without trying to alert Marisa, or alarm her for that matter, Tyler pushed them faster than usual before making camp.

Since the day they'd crossed the bridge, both he and Marisa had made certain to keep their distance from each other. When he'd set camp, she'd do some magic with the fruits and plants she managed to gather while they'd hiked. He didn't know what she did to the stuff, but it was edible, some of it even tasty. It wasn't fish, and along with the protein bars that were nearly gone, it was enough to keep their energy going.

When they talked, they both seemed to tacitly agree to stay away from the subject of El Jefe and *la Fortuna*.

He learned about the interpreting projects she did on the side, but found it difficult to picture her wearing a pink waitress uniform, serving up coffee and flapjacks at her other job. He also figured she must have been little more than a teenager when she'd met the creep she'd almost married.

He, on the other hand, told her about life in Mission Creek. About the two families—the Carsons and the Wainwrights—who were the backbone of the town, and the guys he usually played a round of golf with on Sunday mornings when he wasn't out on assignment.

Her eyebrows had nearly skyrocketed when, at her skepticism, he'd insisted that his foursome really had found a baby there at the LSCC. The foursome that Luke would have been a part of if he hadn't been down in Mezcaya trying to fight his way to Westin. Now, Luke was injured and pretty much in shock that the baby they'd found could possibly be his.

When Marisa had commented on Tyler's unusual talkativeness, he'd shrugged it off. How could he admit that by revealing something of himself, he'd been hoping she'd do the same? That she'd give him some understanding of the real reason she was in on the mission to save Westin. All he ended up doing, though, was grow more curious about her.

The farther they trekked, the more he wondered about that shadow, deep in her eyes, that seemed to become darker with each mile. Was it because they were nearing El Jefe's territory? Or was it for some other reason?

He didn't know.

But he did know that he had to deal with their tracker. And soon. Another day wouldn't pass before the guy would be on to them.

"We'll stop here for the day," he announced, knowing Marisa was puzzled, but also knowing that she was exhausted and not likely to argue. "It's a good spot. You can get, uh, a shower."

Halting beside Tyler, Marisa slid off the daypack.

Her glance slid to the sight just ahead. "It's a waterfall," she said. Then she flushed at the absurdity of it. Of course, he knew that. The spray of the falls cast such a fine mist that it nearly reached where they stood in a grassy clearing, about fifty yards away. "Did you know we were coming up on it?"

"Is that a polite way of asking if we're lost?"

She couldn't quite manage a smile. She was too tired. And whether or not *he* knew where they were, *she* certainly did. Now.

She and her brothers and sisters had played too many days under that very waterfall for her not to recognize it.

"Not at all," she assured faintly. If they were this close to the falls, then they were within miles of her parents' home. And definitely not heading toward *la Fortuna.*

The realization made her dizzy and she swayed. Tyler, darn him, noticed and took it for hunger, for he nudged her down to sit on the pack he'd pulled from his own back.

"Eat a protein bar," he ordered flatly.

"We only have one left." Again, she stated the obvious, for he had already pulled the thing from her daypack.

He tore open the wrapping and practically stuck it in her face. "Eat it."

She turned her head away. But she did take the

bar and break off a chunk. Then she handed him the rest. "I will, if you will."

His expression didn't change. But he didn't argue and he did take the remainder of the bar. "I'm going to check out the trail for tomorrow," he said. "You stay here." He handed her the machete. "Keep that with you."

Her stomach tightened even more. The bite of protein bar sat uncomfortably as suspicion's ugly head reared even higher. "Why?"

"We need to get to *la Fortuna* soon."

"Tell me something I don't know," she said slowly. "What's wrong?"

"Nothing."

It didn't matter that she'd known this man for barely a week. They'd spent hour after hour after hour in each other's company and she knew his expressions—what few he'd let show.

She knew when he was laughing inside, like when she'd screamed the previous morning upon finding a tiny lizard that had crawled inside her shoe during the night. A small crease had formed alongside his mobile lips.

She knew when he was hurting, because his face went devoid of expression altogether.

She knew when he was thinking about that kiss, because the line of his jaw went even tighter and his dark eyes even darker.

And right now, she knew he was lying.

Something was wrong, and it wasn't the bruise on his ribcage, it wasn't their dwindling supplies, it wasn't anything that they'd been dealing with as they'd climbed up mountains and descended into valleys.

She just didn't quite know what to do about it. So she sat there, watching him retie his bootlaces and strap a small hunting knife to his belt. "You've never checked out the trail in advance before."

His grunt was noncommittal. And it worried her even more.

"Tyler—"

"Consider it a reprieve from my company for an hour or two. I'm sure you'll enjoy that," he said easily. "I'll be back before it's dark."

Her teeth worried the inside of her lip, and she pushed to her feet. She dashed a lock of hair from her eyes. "What if you're not?"

"Start dinner without me." His grin was faint.

"Ha-ha. I like 'stay in the boat' better," she said, mimicking his deep voice.

At that, he did smile. Fully enough that it displayed dimples she'd have never known he possessed. Deep, slashing dimples that she could see despite the dark whiskers shadowing his jaw.

It was mesmerizing, she realized faintly. Seeing

Tyler Murdoch smile. "How old are you, Murdoch?"

"Thirty-five, and feeling every damn day of it. Why?"

She lifted her shoulder. "You just should smile more often."

"Now you sound like a woman."

Her head tilted. "Well, I am."

"Trust me, M. I noticed that." He took a step away from her.

"Tyler—" She didn't understand the urgency that spurred her. But she reached out, caught his arm between her hands. "I do trust you." And she realized, as she said the words, that it was true. Whether he believed in her or not, it didn't affect her trust in him. Somewhere along the way, between river rapids, rotting bridges and miles of nearly impassible jungle, she'd begun to trust. And maybe it was just that fact alone that put such a sense of unease in her. "Come back. Okay?"

He brushed his thumb over her chin. "I'm only checking the trail. I won't leave you."

She moistened her lips. She truly didn't understand the nerves slowly choking her. "You promise? You're not going to *la Fortuna* without me?"

A muscle in his jaw ticked. His eyes narrowed. "Who are you, M.?"

The question should have struck her as odd, yet

didn't. "I'm Marisa Elisa Santiago de Rodriguez," she whispered. "Native of Mezcaya. Former translator. Current hiking companion." She swallowed again. "You promise you'll come back?"

"Yes."

She forced a smile and let go of his arm. "Well, then, go do your thing. I...I'm going to have that shower." She plucked at the T-shirt she was wearing. "Freshen up a little. Dress for dinner, you know. I thought we'd go formal tonight, for our figs and mangos."

He didn't smile. "Keep the machete with you."

She nodded, words failing her. Then he was walking away, moving fast down the barely visible trail. And Marisa, keeping the machete close at hand, dragged the backpacks closer to the mist-shrouded pool at the base of the waterfall.

It was a long while, though, before she finally undressed and waded into the mist.

Because if Tyler really were checking the trail ahead, then why had he left the binoculars behind?

"I don't think it was a good idea to come here," Josie Lavender Carson murmured as she and her husband, Flynt, entered the Yellow Rose Café at the Lone Star Country Club.

Flynt helped her seat her very pregnant self. "Staying around the house, making yourself crazy staring at the phone isn't gonna bring Lena back any quicker, Josie. The FBI is doing everything it can to find her kidnappers.''

The tears that came so easily these days flooded Josie's eyes and she clung to her husband's hand as he sat down beside her. She'd never been so grateful in her whole life that she had this strong man's love as she had been since the day she'd gone in to check on the baby at naptime, only to find her missing.

Flynt's hand covered hers. He pressed his lips to her forehead and gently shushed her. With a subtle shake of his head, he steered off the waitress who'd been heading for their table. His brother, Matt, was supposed to be meeting them for lunch.

''We'll get Lena back, Josie. I promise you.'' It wasn't the first time he'd said the words in the last few days.

She moistened her lips, struggling for control. ''Every time I close my eyes, all I can see is that sweet baby girl. I'd put that red bow in her hair that morning. It's her favorite, I swear it is. Her eyes light up like sapphires whenever she sees it. And it looks so perfect with her dark hair.''

Flynt murmured. ''I know.''

''What if whoever took her doesn't know how she loves peaches and loathes peas? What if she goes hungry?''

"She won't," Flynt assured gently, though they both knew he had no way of knowing for certain.

Seventy-two hours ago somebody had waltzed into the Carson ranch and snatched, right out from under their noses, the baby who'd found her way into all their hearts. It sent a cold fury right down to Flynt's soul. It didn't matter that the little mite wasn't his.

Finding Lena the way they had that day on the golf course of the Lone Star Country Club had been the start of living again as far as Flynt was concerned.

There they'd been. Flynt, Tyler Murdoch, Spence Harrison and Michael O'Day who'd been filling in for Luke Callaghan that day. Teeing off on the ninth hole. Tyler had been trying to take bets on him having the longest drive and Spence had been challenging it when they'd heard the unmistakable sound of a baby.

The sight of the carrier and the baby inside it near the bushes had stunned them all into silence. The note that had been pinned to the blanket had been hardly legible thanks to water dripping from the bushes. But it had been enough to know the baby belonged to one of 'em. It had been enough to know the mother was nowhere in sight, though they'd done their share of searching.

And since then, since Flynt had decided to take

care of the munchkin while they figured out who was really her father and maybe, just maybe, who was the mother who'd been so desperate to leave her child that way, his life had started anew.

For Lena had led him to Josie, and Josie was his life now. Her and the baby growin' inside her. And until the identity of Lena's real father was determined, it was Flynt's duty—hell, it was his privilege—to raise Lena like his own.

Flynt had already lost one family. He wasn't about to lose one single member of the one he had now.

"We're gonna find Lena," he assured his wife once again. And he had a good idea just where to start.

The Wainwrights.

Which was why Matt was meeting them for lunch today. Because his bride, Rose, was a member of that family. And while Flynt didn't necessarily have a thing against Rose, who seemed to be doing a bang-up job of keeping a grin on his kid brother's face, he wouldn't trust any other member of that family as far as he could throw 'em.

The Carsons and the Wainwrights had been feuding since their grandparents' day, and as far as Flynt was concerned, it would be just like that damn stubborn Archy Wainwright to be at the root of Lena's disappearance no matter what the FBI had said about the unlikelihood of that.

Josie's hands were twisting together again on top of the table. He covered them with his hands and waved over the waitress who was bearing a tray loaded with fresh water and coffee.

"Afternoon, Daisy," Flynt greeted the pretty blonde when she came over to the table. "We're expecting Matt, too."

The waitress smiled and set out several glasses of water. "Would y'all like menus today or do you already have your minds set?"

"Flynt, I really don't think I can eat a thing," Josie murmured beside him. "Honestly, you could have left me at home."

"Where you'd work yourself into a worried tizzy. No, I want you with me, so I can take care of you." He glanced up at Daisy who seemed to be doing her best not to eavesdrop while she stood near his elbow. "My wife'll have a glass of milk and the small chicken salad. Bring it on out anytime. But I'll wait until Matt gets here to order. I'll take some coffee now, though, if that pot you've got there is fresh."

"Flynt "

"Josie, you have to think of yourself and our baby, too. Neglecting yourself is not going to find Lena any faster." His quick hand caught the empty coffee mug that tumbled from Daisy's tray before it could hit anything.

"I'm sorry," Daisy murmured, distressed. "I

couldn't help… Lena? Something's happened to the baby?''

Flynt sighed. Beyond Daisy's slender figure he saw Matt and Rose enter the restaurant. ''Yes, Lena has been kidnapped.'' Just saying the words made him feel ill.

Daisy looked horrified. She blinked, murmured something about more menus and hurried away just before Matt helped a very pregnant Rose slide into the booth, much the same way Flynt had just done with Josie. Rose was due to deliver shortly.

''No news, yet,'' Rose surmised with one look at Josie's face. Josie shook her head silently. Rose sighed, her face troubled. ''I know your daddy thinks mine had something to do with this,'' she told Flynt. ''Ford called, accusing my father of being at the bottom of it.'' She ignored the telling look Matt and Flynt shared, ''I know our families have had their troubles, but they wouldn't do this.''

Another waitress came by, filling Matt's and Flynt's mugs with coffee. ''For your sake, Rose, I hope you're right.''

Tyler didn't waste time feeling guilty for lying to Marisa as he ducked off the minimal trail and rapidly moved through the thick of the forest back toward Blondie. Branches and palms scratched at his arms and face, but he didn't feel them. He almost wished he'd had a firearm, but maybe it was better that he didn't.

He was a good shot, but he wasn't a crack shot.

What he *was,* was a genius when it came to explosives which didn't exactly fall into the realm of hand-to-hand. And since the Gulf, he'd spent more and more of his time on the intelligence end of things, traveling the world, consulting, conducting meetings and generally spreading his knowledge where it was most needed. Nevertheless, he was making good time as he jogged through the forest.

Birds scattered by the dozens as he passed by their perches, and in the corner of his eye, he caught the tail of some big cat. It was a wonder that he and Marisa hadn't had more encounters with the wildlife than they had. Aside from the snake and a few lizards, they'd been pretty well left alone.

Except for Blondie, there.

He figured he'd run a good three miles when he got close enough to the tracker's camp to smell the guy's campfire. Sucking in air, he silently made his way closer. "A cliff dweller," he muttered as he neared. For Blondie seemed to have made his camp near the edge of a canyon similar to the one that he and Marisa had crossed days earlier.

A cliff dweller…and what else?

Tyler had dismissed the supposition that Blondie was some local guy protecting his turf after the guy had followed them for a few days. They'd simply zigzagged over too much ground for that.

A part of him hoped he'd find the guy to just be a poacher, hunting out of season, on land where he shouldn't be. Or some overgrown hippie who was out living off the land, smoking dope in the privacy of the jungle.

But his gut told him otherwise.

When he stepped into the clearing and saw the arsenal of weapons Blondie possessed, Tyler knew his gut had, once again, been right on the money.

"Looking for me?" he asked pleasantly and swiftly kicked the rifle right out of Blondie's hands. He was sick of playing cat and mouse, and he wanted answers. He took the guy down, hard and fast. "You messed up my plane, you jackass," he muttered as he pinned the guy to the ground. "I oughta kill you just for that."

"You try," the other man grunted. His voice was thick with an accent.

German, Tyler thought. Thanks to Marisa's propensity for muttering in other languages behind his back, he was actually learning something. He pressed his arm even harder against his windpipe. "Who sent you?"

The other man laughed, harsh and breathy from the pressure on his throat. "No one sends me," he assured arrogantly. With a quick twist, he managed to clip Tyler's jaw hard enough to make his head snap back.

And there the niceties ended. It wasn't pretty and it wasn't graceful. Blondie knew how to fight. And when he couldn't seem to take down Tyler with his fists, he knew how to run.

But Tyler wasn't having any of that. When Blondie headed toward the edge of the cliff, Tyler followed. He dived and tackled the German from behind, and their bodies careened toward the edge. Tyler grabbed a root and halted their progress, locking his arm around the German's neck. "I asked," he repeated, his voice soft, deadly, "who sent you?"

"You drug-runners. Each one I bring in, El Jefe pay me." The German's fingers scrabbled for Tyler's face, his eyes.

The gravelly ground beneath them shifted dangerously. "You work for El Jefe."

"I work for no one. El Jefe pay me. Don't invade their territory," the man gasped. "They pay well. You are nothing but a stupid American, flying your fancy little plane down here to score."

"Every time you mention my plane," Tyler said, "you piss me off." He dug his heels into the ground, halting another slide. "You've been following me and my friend, and that pisses me off. Basically—" he squeezed a fraction tighter "—*you* piss me off."

The German swore at him and struggled against

the headlock. His feet went over the edge and Tyler yanked back. "Not so fast."

But the momentum was too much, and his hold loosened. Just enough. And suddenly, the German was dangling over the cliff. Tyler grabbed his shirt, his shoulders, hanging on for all he was worth.

"Don't drop me!" The German scrabbled for the edge, his voice suddenly panicked. "Sell your drugs, do whatever. Is nothing to me."

"I don't believe you," Tyler gritted, as every muscle in his body strained. Centimeter by centimeter he pulled. Blondie was almost as tall as he was, and it was no easy task. Particularly with the way the guy was swinging his legs back and forth in a panic to get back on firm ground.

Some piece of his mind imagined hauling Blondie along as a prisoner. They couldn't spare the time to leave him off with any authorities that Tyler could afford to trust. Having a prisoner would slow their progress to *la Fortuna,* but it would also ensure the guy couldn't warn El Jefe before Tyler could get there.

Finally, finally, he'd pulled the other man up enough for Tyler to reach down and grab the man by the belt. He hauled, groaning out loud at the effort.

It took him a minute to feel the pain.

But when he did, it was fierce. A burning, awful,

deadly pain. Feeling stupid, slow, he looked down to see the wicked gleam in the other man's eyes as he pulled out the blade he'd just sliced into Tyler's shoulder.

Blood gushed from the wound, running down his arm. His fingers went numb. He wasn't even aware of letting go of his hold on the German. But he was fully aware of the man crawling over the edge, knife aloft.

"El Jefe pay whether you dead or alive. And with you dead, the girl be even easier to kill."

Tyler's blood went cold. Using every bit of strength left in him, he swept the German's leg hard. The man stumbled, cartwheeled.

And disappeared over the edge.

Tyler fell back against the ground and stared up into the blue sky. The clouds were racing around in dizzying circles. "Ah, hell," he muttered. He did not have time to pass out. But he had to close his eyes. Just for a minute. Just until the dizziness eased up. And then he'd get to Marisa and tell her

He frowned, his thoughts drifting. Tell her what?

"By dark, he said." Marisa paced, following the circumference of light cast by the fire she'd started. "Won't leave you, he said." For the hundredth time, she stopped, staring into the darkness beyond, listening fiercely for the sound, any sound, that Tyler was returning.

Nothing.

She'd bathed in the waterfall and coaxed a fire into burning. She'd snared a fish, cleaned it, cooked it and eaten it.

And still. Nothing.

Tears threatened, but she refused to give in to them. She should have followed her instincts and followed after Tyler when there had still been some light to guide her way.

And now, even the moon seemed to be hiding in that expanse of endless black overhead. Guarding its cool, white light, too selfish to share when Marisa most needed it.

She didn't know how much time was passing. But it seemed an agony of long, hard heartbeats as she paced. And paced.

And paced.

Finally she could take it no longer. She'd just have to take her own illumination because she couldn't wait for Tyler one more minute. She had to do something, or go insane.

She felt around for a large, substantial branch. The best she could find was one about as thick as her arm. She stuck it straight into the fire, afraid the green wood wouldn't catch. When it finally did, she turned to face the void beyond the fire, beyond the tumble of the waterfall, beyond the misty air that made her hair curl into ringlets around her shoulders.

But she'd taken only one step into that void when something came crashing through the brush. Startled, Marisa backed toward the firelight.

And then Tyler was there. He grinned faintly when he saw her. "Hi, honey, I'm home."

Her jaw dropped. And adrenaline raced through her when his eyes seemed to roll back in his head and he pitched forward, falling flat on the ground.

Her shocked paralysis lasted only a millisecond before she dropped the branch into the fire and darted forward, desperately running her hands over his body, carefully turning him onto his side. On his back. She felt the wetness, saw the blood on her hands in the firelight. Chanting his name like a litany, she scrabbled for T-shirts, for anything to stanch the blood seeping from his shoulder. She finally used her teeth to help rip one of his cotton shirts into strips that she bound around him, creating a tourniquet of sorts.

His forehead was cold, clammy. His pulse rapid.

And what she knew about first-aid would have fit on the head of a pin. No amount of effort seemed to penetrate his unconsciousness. He was out cold. Probably from losing so much blood.

Containing her panic by mere threads, she went to the pool and washed off the blood and made herself not think about infections and germs and the fact that they were miles from any sort of help, and she dare not leave him in the middle of the night, wounded as he was, anyway.

She didn't know how he'd been injured, or by whom or what, and she didn't know whether that danger was still out there. So she did the only thing she could. She crouched down and tucked her arms beneath Tyler's muscled shoulders, wincing when he seemed to groan. Inch by aching inch, she dragged his big body closer to the warmth and sense of safety provided by the small fire. When she finally managed it, she fell back, breathing hard.

With the site of his wound better illuminated, Marisa could see the dark stain spreading through the bundled shirts, and she hurriedly found another. How much blood could a man lose?

Enough to die.

The thought hung in the back of her mind, like some hideous, evil thing.

Marisa ignored it. She replaced one sodden padding after another. And finally, oh, yes, finally, after what seemed hours, the bleeding slowed.

And when dawn was breaking over the horizon, it stopped altogether, giving her a chance to finally wash the blood from the cloths in the falls and spread them out to dry.

Driven by nerves and fear, Marisa regularly cradled his head in her arm, urging small sips of water from the canteen. His clamminess had been replaced, sometime during those dark hours, with fever, and now his skin felt hot. His head twisted against her gentle touch, his good arm thrashing out at her as his voice, rough and barely understandable, railed at some unseen person.

Afraid he'd disturb the wound and start bleeding again, she lay beside him, holding his arms still, trying to calm him. He just swore at her, low and guttural. Eventually his eyes opened, glassy and fevered. He called her "Sonya," then lapsed into unconsciousness again. Marisa wanted to weep for the agony in his expression.

She dissolved the last few aspirin in the water, desperate to get it in his system, and succeeded only partially. By the time the sun hung high in the sky, she knew she couldn't wait any longer. Tyler needed more help than she could possibly provide on her own. There was no denying it. His condition was worsening.

If only she could remember the plants and roots that her mother and grandmother had used to heal every complaint from headaches to indigestion to deep, gaping slashes.

Leaving him sheltered from the sun by the tarp that she strung over him as best she could, she folded

the rinsed and dried T-shirts and carefully peeled
away the used ones from his wound.

"La madre de Dios." The sight of the cut was
horrible. Worse than she'd expected. She had to
swallow down a wave of nausea. "Fight against this,
Tyler," she said fiercely as she gently, carefully
placed the impromptu bandages over the gash.
"Westin needs you." She tied off the bandages and
stared into his face. They'd both gotten more tan
over the past several days, yet his skin was ashen
beneath that. His lashes lay thick and unbearably
vulnerable against the deep circles beneath his eyes.
What she wouldn't give for a healthy dose of his
impossible confidence right now. *"I* need you," she
whispered.

Feeling even more urgent, she continued talking,
telling him, again and again, as she packed cool, wet
cloths around his body and urged him to drink just
a little more water, that she'd return with help.

She prayed that he'd understand her. She prayed
that she wasn't putting him in more danger by leaving. She prayed that she would remember the way.

And if she did remember, she prayed that her family wouldn't turn her away.

Eight

"Tia Marisa," the small voice asked, "will you make my hair pretty like yours?"

Tyler swallowed. Opening his eyes felt like too damn much work, so he just lay there, listening to the soft murmur of voices—one a child's, one lower and more melodious—as he took stock.

There was a blanket over him, coarse and vaguely itchy. Whatever he was lying on, it was comfortable enough. Little too soft for his taste. But, then, he'd been used to sleeping on the ground lately—

His eyes opened, a demand on his lips that came out more like a croak.

Marisa's gaze shifted from the pretty little blond girl sitting on her lap to him. Her eyes widened when she saw he was awake, and with a quiet murmur, she set the child aside and stepped over to the bed. "*Esté tranquilo,*" she whispered, touching his shoulders lightly. "Be still." She reached for something and a small cup entered his vision.

She slipped her arm, strong and supportive, under

his neck and lifted slightly as she held the water to his mouth. "Go easy, Tyler. You're very weak."

He drank, greedy, impatient. And not so weak that he wasn't aware of the soft press of her breasts as she leaned over him, settling him back against the thin pillow. He closed his eyes for a minute, and when he opened them, she was still sitting there, arms folded against the too-soft bed.

Her almond-shaped eyes were the same ones they'd always been, but this Marisa looked different from any that he'd met before. She didn't look the elegant, uppity linguistics expert dressed in ivory linen and leather shoes. Nor was she the fey jungle creature, wearing a sleeveless T-shirt and sweatpants hacked off at the knee with a knife, sporting dirt on her face and laughter in her eyes as she talked him into just tasting the barbecued banana.

Now her gleaming hair hung loose in waves around her shoulders, and the dress she wore was so vivid with a half-dozen bright colors that it almost made him dizzy. Yet she was Marisa. He'd recognize her eyes, that touch, that warm, soft scent of hers, no matter what the circumstance.

He recognized her, but he sure in hell didn't recognize where they were. The room was simply structured. The big square window opposite the bed looked like it had no glass in it, but there were shutters—currently opened—that would provide protection against the night and the weather. Behind the stool where Marisa sat, there was a doorway, though he couldn't see where it led. Into another room, maybe. It was a house, clearly. Clean and airy, from what he could tell, but hardly luxurious.

He moved, running one hand experimentally across his chest. He felt thick wads of bandages. Then he remembered the German. And the knife.

"Where are we?" His voice sounded rusty, unused, and he felt unease slice through him. "How long—"

"Shh," she pressed her fingertips lightly to his lips. "You're safe. It's been a few days."

He caught her fingers and could tell she was surprised by the strength with which he gripped her. "How many days?"

Her lips tightened. "A week, Tyler. It's been a week."

He swore, and tried to sit up. "Where's the backpack?"

But she planted her hands on his shoulders and gently pushed him right back down. "It's here, Tyler. Everything is here, I promise you. But you're not going to undo the good work my *abuela* has done," she said flatly. "Now be still."

"Where am I?"

Her lashes fell, hiding her expression from him. "We are at my parents' home. I told them there was a problem with your plane and we had to crash land.'' She looked over her shoulder when she heard a clatter of noises and voices nearing. ''Tyler, they think that you're my hu—''

''Marisa, *mi niña*.'' A tall woman who could only be Marisa's mother entered the room, her hands buried in the white apron wrapped around her slender waist. ''You did not tell me your husband was awake at last.'' The woman's English was heavily accented, but clear. As clear as the disapproval she directed at her daughter.

Tyler looked from the woman to Marisa who was staring at him, a near-pleading expression in her eyes. She moistened her lips and looked over her shoulder. ''I'm sorry, Mama. He just now awakened.'' Then she looked back at Tyler, with something that looked very much like regret in her eyes.

She wrapped her hands around his, and he wondered who was the sick one, because her hands were positively cold and clammy. ''Tyler, this is my mother. Belicia.''

Tyler nodded at the woman who was watching him with a wide smile. ''Ma'am,'' he murmured, not quite sure what to say. It was one thing to pretend to be married to penetrate *la Fortuna,* but to lie about it to Marisa's mother?

The woman looked at her daughter and a spate of Spanish words flew from her lips, making color rise in Marisa's long, lovely throat. She glanced at him hurriedly, then back to her mother. "*Sí,* I am very fortunate. He is very handsome." Her cheeks went even duskier when Belicia continued talking and gesturing.

Catching about every tenth word, if that, Tyler got the distinct impression that his masculinity was being very thoroughly dissected, and he didn't know whether to close his eyes and pretend he wasn't there, or to make sure the blanket covered him from head to toe, because he was pretty sure he was naked as a jaybird under the rough cloth.

Then Marisa hopped up and began maneuvering her mother from the room. She quickly pulled down the vividly woven mat that sufficed for a door and then turned to face Tyler. Only she looked everywhere but at him as she folded her arms across her middle.

"You grew up here?" His voice came a little more naturally.

She nodded. "Until they let me go live with a cousin in Belize when I was thirteen. I begged to attend school there." She walked around the small confines of the room, and he could feel the waves of tension rolling off her. "I was the eldest, you see. And my parents, they wanted me to—" She broke off, pressing her fingertips to her forehead. "My brothers looked for the person who stabbed you, but they found no one.''

"He's dead," Tyler said flatly, remembering the look on the German's face as he'd gone over the edge of the cliff. It wasn't the first time he'd had to kill or be killed. But it didn't mean he liked it. "Your parents wanted you to what?"

Marisa's shoulders seemed to sag a little. "I was so worried." She felt for the stool and sat beside him again. Still, she wouldn't look him in the face. "I didn't know if we'd be followed here, but you needed help and…" She shook her head, pressing her lips together. Almost absently, she offered the water cup to Tyler again, helping him drink, before setting it aside once more. "I recognized the waterfall, you see. I knew we were near here."

Which explained how she'd gotten him here, but didn't finish at all what she'd been saying about her parents.

"I hated leaving you," she added. "But it was necessary."

"Necessary things aren't always easy," he said. "It doesn't matter, Marisa. We're both still alive. The guy tracking us is dead. And the sooner I'm on my feet, the quicker I'll get to Westin."

Her fingers plucked at a loose thread on the blanket. "You said his name a lot. In your fever." She hesitated. "And someone named Sonya." Her lashes lifted for a quick glance his way, then dropped again to shield her expression. "And Lena. My mother, she, um, she heard. She thinks you have too many mistresses and that I brought you to Mezcaya to prove I am woman enough to satisfy you."

His jaw loosened. He wasn't a particularly talkative man, but he was rarely speechless. "I…what?"

She covered her face with her hand. "Please don't make me repeat it, Murdoch. It's embarrassing enough."

"Lena's the baby I told you about," he muttered, lying back on the pillow. How had this mission gone so damned awry? "The one my buddies and I found on the golf course."

"Is…is she yours?" The words came out in a rush. "And Sonya's?"

"Hell no!" He jerked up, winced and lay back. "Well, we don't know for certain who the kid's father is yet. But I was pretty sure she wasn't mine even before it was ruled out by a DNA test. I don't go around acting like Johnny Appleseed."

"Johnny Appleseed?"

The reference had escaped her. "Spreading my seed wherever I go," he said, irritated with the entire subject.

Her cheeks went red all over again. She nibbled her lip for a moment. "Well, that's, um, good."

Tyler knew she was leading up to asking about

Sonya, and he just didn't want to go there. "What was it your parents wanted you to do?"

She popped up and smoothed her hand down the blanket. "You really should get some rest, Tyler. I'll come check on you in a while. Perhaps you'll be up to having some soup. My *abuela* does most of the cooking here. She doesn't like to share her kitchen, not even with my mother. Everything she makes is good, though." She smiled quickly. "She'll leave out the chilies for you. At least until you are healed. Then she'll lay them on hot and heavy so you can prove your manhood."

"We've got hot peppers in Texas, honey."

Marisa just smiled as she headed for the exit. And Tyler didn't trust that smile for a minute. Joking or not, he wasn't sure he wanted to find out. He also noticed that she hadn't answered his question.

"Why'd you tell them I was your husband?" His voice was quiet. He didn't want the question to carry.

She paused in the act of pulling aside the mat. "Because it's the only way they'd forgive me," she said after a moment. Then she ducked through the doorway and was gone.

"I have to do something!" Haley Mercado aka Daisy Parker raked back her blonde hair with hands that trembled. "She's my baby. It's not right!"

Sean Collins, the FBI agent assigned to her case, stood square in the doorway of the office. "You cannot come out of hiding. Everything that can be done to find Lena is being done. Don't let that distract you from our task here."

Haley stared at the man in disbelief. "My *daughter*," she snapped with fury, "has been kidnapped and you don't want me to be *distracted*?"

He had the grace to look apologetic. "I know this is difficult for you. But you've come so far. We're so close. We need the final details of the smuggling scheme. And you're the only one who can get them for us if we're finally going to put the Texas mob on ice."

"She'll have her first birthday on March 15," Haley whispered, hardly listening to Sean. Her arms ached to hold her baby girl again. The past months of seeing her at a distance whenever Josie brought the baby by the LSCC had barely sustained her. But she'd comforted herself with the knowledge that her daughter was being very well cared for, and was safe. "Haven't I given up enough," she asked, not really expecting an answer. "My mother is dead. God knows where Ricky is now. And Luke—" she couldn't continue.

"Lena will be found," Sean said again. "But if you come out of hiding now, when she *is* found, she may not have a mother still alive to come home to."

Haley sank down on the chair and buried her face in her hands. She'd never felt more alone in her life.

Would this nightmare never end?

After a few days of recuperating, Tyler was impatient to be up and around. Since he'd regained consciousness, he'd met a parade of people who were Marisa's relations. Brothers. Cousins. Sisters. Nieces. Nephews. Her grandmother, who didn't speak a lick of English, was one of the few people around who didn't look at him as if he were an oddity from another planet.

Maybe because she'd been the one to sponge his naked body when he'd been in a tearing fever.

Even now, it nearly made him cringe to think of the tiny, wizened old woman doing that. Worse, to know that Marisa, as his "wife" had been the other to tend to him while he'd been out of it.

He didn't have a problem being naked with Marisa. He just wished he'd been more aware of it, so he might have enjoyed it a little more. His lips twisted at the thought.

Instead Marisa had slept on a floor mat beside his bed every night. In the morning she'd stow the mat and rumple "her" side of the bed, to make it appear as if they'd slept together.

It was enough to drive a sane man around the

bend, all this focus on whether or not his "wife" shared his bed.

But, maybe he'd already gone around the bend before Marisa had weaseled her seductive way into the center of his thoughts. Even now, sitting on a metal folding chair, of all things, located at the rear of the house that overlooked the fields—vegetables for their own family and those in the village and sugarcane that they sold at market—he couldn't help wondering where she was. What she was doing.

And he couldn't blame it on the fact that he'd been miles off in his estimation of the life that she'd grown up with. He'd watched her with her family and as he'd done so, he'd gained a little understanding. Not because he understood a hell of a lot of what they said. But some things went beyond language.

And this Mezcayan family, who'd been untraditional enough to allow their eldest child—Marisa—to go off to school in neighboring Belize where the educational system was much more advanced than Mezcaya's, was rigidly traditional when it came to the "duties" of its family members. Which seemed to be, namely, getting married and having lots of babies. And as far as Tyler could tell, aside from Inez who was still a teenager, Marisa was the only one to have not fulfilled that expectation.

The only thing that Tyler wasn't quite sure of was where Marisa's goals fit into the picture.

The fact that he was even interested in what Marisa's goals were should have yanked on his reins but good. What the hell did it matter to him? He was just stuck with her company on this mission.

Unfortunately the declaration wasn't ringing quite as true as he'd like.

Then his senses picked up Marisa behind him before she even spoke. "You've been up nearly all day today," she said. "Perhaps you should rest now."

He looked back to see she was carrying a plump, toothless baby on her hip. He figured he ought to know which sibling the child belonged to, but he didn't. Busying his mind on figuring that out was wiser than letting his attention focus too hard on Marisa.

She'd obviously borrowed some clothes from someone; maybe her younger sister, Inez. Which would account for the brief denim shorts that were a little too loose in the hips, and the skimpy red top that was a little too snug.

Even in this secluded corner of Mezcaya, fashion for teenaged girls was apparently alive and well.

"I've rested enough," he said and deliberately looked away from Marisa's bare legs. He was about to climb out of his skin from being so inactive for so long. He didn't want to think about what other reason he had for being so restless.

"You're anxious to be on your way."

There was little point in denying it. "I'm healing up." If he didn't have to haul anyone up a cliff face, he figured he'd be fine. And if he did have to haul someone, he figured he'd manage. He saw the skepticism in her eyes. "Your faith in my ability is heartwarming, M."

"You'll accomplish anything you set out to do. I have no doubts about that. But you *are* still healing."

Tyler looked out across the rich fields. "I guarantee you I'm in better shape than Westin is. And every hour that passes—" He didn't finish. There was no need to.

Marisa sighed faintly. She touched his shoulder, a fleeting touch before she was moving away, putting more distance between them as she jiggled the baby. He wondered if she was thinking about that day when she'd practically torn off his shirt in her drive to touch him.

"You look good with a kid on your hip," he said abruptly.

Her lips stretched into a smile and she nuzzled the baby's neck. "Nicholas is a darling, isn't he?"

"As far as kids go," he said.

She looked at him, amusement making her eyes

dance. He didn't think he'd ever met anyone whose expressions were so revealing.

"Oh, Murdoch. Don't you ever want to be— What did you call it? Johnny Appleseed."

He shrugged. "Kids are a lot of responsibility."

"And a lot of joy."

He had a brief flash of his own childhood. "Not for everybody."

Her gaze seemed to go inward for a moment and her amusement faded. "Yes. That is very true."

"Why aren't you settled with a bunch of bambinos? Didn't the madman want kids?"

He couldn't tell what she thought about him bringing up her ex-fiancé. "The only things my ex wanted were power and control," she said with a practiced shrug.

"And you." He didn't know why he kept at it. "He wanted you."

Her lips twisted. "Well, he certainly didn't want anyone else to want me."

"Possessive sort."

"That's one word for it." She shifted the baby around and grinned into his cherubic face, making it clear that she didn't intend to say more on the subject. "If you don't want to laze around, then maybe you'd like to go out for a walk."

"Are you talking to the toothless wonder there, or to me?"

"Take your pick," she said. "Either way, I'll have a handsome fellow accompanying me." She cast him a half smiling, apologetic look as she continued, "My mama tells me that I've been neglecting my husband while we've been here, and that I should lure you out for some exercise."

"The kind that would put a baby in your belly?" He shrugged when she gaped at him. "Inez talks a lot when she's bored. She said your parents and grandmother think a baby is just what we need to keep my attentions where they belong. I gotta say, M., that your family doesn't hesitate to share its opinions."

Marisa closed her eyes. The next time she saw Inez, she'd have a hard time not throttling the girl. She'd come to expect such comments from her mother and father, even her *abuela* on occasion. But from her baby sister? "I'm sorry if she embarrassed you."

Tyler laughed softly, and Marisa went still, unable to believe she was actually hearing laughter coming from his lips. "Smiles and now laughter? Murdoch, if I didn't know better, I might think you actually are relaxing here."

"Well, *mi esposa,* there is relaxed, and then there's relaxed." His gaze was deceptively lazy, reminding her of a big languid cat rhythmically swishing his tail, looking for all the world as if he were content to endlessly lie in the sun, when in reality he was only biding his time until the perfect moment to strike.

Her stomach tightened and to distract herself, she tickled Nicholas's neck, making the baby gurgle and grin. "You probably shouldn't be out traipsing around, anyway, no matter what they say." Keeping her voice calm was no small task. "If you go lie down, I'll bring you some juice."

"I'm not five years old with a tummy ache," he countered dryly. He rose from the chair, reminding her yet again of that big dangerous cat.

Marisa moistened her lips and jiggled Nicholas. His little hands waved around, batting at her arms. "I think Diego is around here somewhere." She'd seen her brother a little earlier. "You could—"

"Give me that kid," Tyler interrupted her, sliding Nicholas out of her arms with an ease she would have never expected. "Before you give him a kidney shake."

Marisa's arms slowly fell to her sides. She watched Tyler plunk Nicholas against his wide, bare chest. The bruising around his ribs had very nearly disappeared. His large hand easily cradled the baby's back, and the baby...well, he was a good-natured little boy, and he seemed fascinated with the unfamiliar man who held him. She barely kept herself from telling him that he, too, looked good with a child in his arms.

Then Tyler held out his hand to Marisa. "Exercise."

She ran her tongue along the edge of her teeth, willing her heartbeat to just settle right back down. "Tyler—"

He knew exactly where her thoughts had gone. She could see it in the humorous glint in his obsidian eyes. "The drooler here can chaperone," he murmured. "Come on. Show me where you ran around as a kid."

She had spent hours with this man, most of them intensely disliking him. So why should she feel as if she'd been presented with an unexpected treat? Her hand trembled faintly when she tentatively took his outstretched one, and she hoped that he didn't notice. "You really must be bored," she commented.

His fingers tightened around hers and he tugged her out from the shade of the house. "Maybe I'm curious about how you got from this—" his chin jerked, encompassing the simple house and all that it implied "—to running around with Gerald Hyde-Smith."

Marisa's feet dragged to an abrupt halt. "I never told you his name." She pulled on her hand, but Tyler's hold was firm. Gentle, but firm.

"Your grandmother did."

"My grandmother's English is about as good as your Mezcayan."

"Oh, the words she surrounded the guy's name with were pretty universal." He tugged until she started walking again with him. "I got the distinct impression she wasn't impressed."

"I wish my parents had been similarly unimpressed." The words were out before Marisa could think. She quickened her step, heading up the small ridge that ran between her family home and the dirt road.

Still, Tyler didn't release her hand. She automatically turned in the direction of the village. The dirt road was hard-packed and rutted from years of rains and droughts and sturdy trucks being driven up and down it by the locals.

"They look at you, Marisa, and it's obvious how proud of you they are. They adore you."

"I don't know why you would even notice such a thing," she said. Besides, she knew how untrue it was. Her mother had made it plain long ago that she was most certainly *not* proud of her when Marisa had wanted to come home after Gerald, and her mother had told her to stay away.

"Noticing things is just one of the things I do."

"And what are the other things you do?" She

quickly waved her free hand. "Never mind. I'm probably not to be trusted with that top-secret stuff."

Tyler tugged her hand, pulling her around to face him there on the road. "I was wrong about that." He wasn't sure when he'd come to that decision. If it was before Blondie had stuck him with the knife, or after. He supposed, in the end, it hardly mattered when. "I'm still not sure about what's really motivating you, but I know you're not—"

"Part of the enemy?" she supplied in a dulcet tone that made him immediately wary.

"Well, yeah."

"And how did you come to this great conclusion? Because I finally proved myself enough to earn your trust while I was blindly traipsing after you as we headed everywhere but toward *la Fortuna?*"

There were times in a man's life when he just knew he was stepping into a mine field. And right then, Tyler figured he must have his foot hovering right over a big ol' Bouncing Betty. And damned if he knew why. "Yeah."

She twisted her wrist, pulling her hand away from his. "I cannot tell you how moved I am." She began walking again. The curling ends of her hair bobbed about her slender waist and dust puffed up around her sandals with each step.

Nicholas patted his jaw. Tyler looked down at the boy. "There is no figuring out women, kid. Accept it now. Save yourself a headache when you get older.''

Nicholas agreed. Tyler could tell by the spit bubble the kid blew.

Tyler headed after Marisa, his longer stride easily catching her. ''You didn't trust me, either, honey,'' he countered flatly. ''So don't get all picky about the reasons why I changed my mind. Hell, you still don't trust me.''

Her lips parted. Her eyes flashed. ''That is so untrue.''

''You're telling me you don't compare me to Hyde-Smith? You don't expect me to behave the same as he did, to pull whatever kind of crap he did that put that wary look in your eyes?''

''You're nothing like Gerald.''

''That's not what you said a week ago.''

''I was wrong!''

''Well, so was I.'' Nicholas fussed, and Tyler realized he was practically yelling. He awkwardly patted the kid's back, hoping he wasn't going to start caterwauling. He lowered his voice. ''Women I've known haven't been real trustworthy, okay? I got so I didn't want to work with them.'' He didn't know why admitting it to her felt like having his skin peeled back. He hadn't made any secret of his opinion about working with women since Sonya turned traitor. ''It spilled over on you. I admit it. I was wrong. Satisfied?'' He realized he was practically jiggling the kid out of his diaper again and deliberately stopped.

''What did she do to you?''

''Who?''

''Sonya.''

''Screwed me and her country over for thirty pieces of silver. It doesn't matter anymore.''

Marisa was staring at him, her eyes wide.

''It doesn't matter anymore,'' he repeated. And knew it was true. Somewhere along the line, Sonya's defection had ceased to hurt. Oh, it was definitely there, angering him that she'd sold them all out. But the piece of him that had been personally wounded, the piece of him that had looked at a woman he'd thought he'd loved yet who'd cared nothing at all in return not for him and sure as hell not for the country she was supposed to be serving—that piece no longer existed.

He looked at Marisa. He was ten years older than she. He'd seen things, lived through things—even done things—that would give most people nightmares. Yet there was something deep down in her eyes that spoke of her own world-weariness, of her own experiences that were none too pretty.

He took a step toward her. And another.

She threw back her head, standing her ground despite the turmoil in her expression. He wondered how she'd come by that ability; if she'd always possessed it, or if it had come at a dear cost.

He lowered his head. Still her gaze remained locked with his. And in her eyes he saw all the things he felt inside.

The tangle of want.

The knowledge that some things were better left untouched.

The awareness that this was something neither could resist reaching for.

Her lips parted softly. He could feel her soft breath, warm on his mouth, bare inches above hers.

"How bad did he hurt you?"

At that, her lashes fell. She took a step back, her head lowered. "He ruined me."

"You're not ruined, Marisa. Not at all. You're too strong."

"If I were, I wouldn't have let him sweep me off my feet the way he did. I would have seen through his charming act to the real person underneath."

"He's assigned to the embassy in D.C.?"

"Not when we met. But yes, eventually. As was I. Until his jealousy cost me my career. And my family." She finally looked up, and Tyler could see the tears that had collected in her eyes. "The only reason my mother didn't turn me away now is because she believes you are my husband. My American husband who is rich enough to have his own plane. It makes up for her embarrassment over my scandalous affairs and subsequent breakup.''

"There were no affairs.''

"Gerald didn't believe that. Every time I had to have any sort of dealing with my co-workers, who were nearly all male, he was suspicious. He wanted me to quit work, to have babies and be the proper little wife. Only, how could I do that when the man never touched me?'' Her throat worked, her cheeks grew red. "He wanted to control everything about me. What I wore. What I said. What I thought. And when I refused to cooperate, when I continued with my work, he spread hideous lies about me.''

The anger that ran through his blood disturbed Tyler. He'd always been a little gung-ho about injustice, but this was more than that. And he couldn't explain it. He couldn't examine the situation, define it, square it away. And he didn't like it.

"Eventually the stories made it back to my parents. My cousin Valencia, the one in Belize, had married into a family with some connections. That's how I was able to go there for school, then a year in the United States before I finished abroad. I met Gerald in London. He proposed quickly because he was being assigned to Washington. I believed him, you see, when he told me he couldn't bear to go without me.'' Her lips twisted. "I was young. Stupid.''

"How long were you together?"

"Eleven months and fourteen days too long," she said flatly. "Things went wrong almost from the start. The very things about me that Gerald had said he'd loved were the very things he complained most about. My accent. My heritage. He didn't even seem to—" She broke off, flushing. "I'm talking too much."

Tyler brushed his thumb over her satiny cheek. "Tell me."

Her throat worked. She closed her eyes. When she opened them, they were full of pain. "He...unless he was upset about something, he couldn't seem to bring himself to touch me. Before long, I didn't want him to, anyway."

The man was a fool as well as a lunatic, Tyler thought. "That's not how it's supposed to be, Marisa." Not that he was any expert on family matters. Not when his own parents hadn't bothered to hang around.

She made a soft sound, blew out a long breath. "Anyway, the rumors that Gerald spread reached my family's ears, thanks to Valencia, and my mother was disgraced. I was their eldest child. Not a male who could take over my father's farm one day. The only thing I was supposed to do was eventually make a good marriage, and in their eyes...well, my mother's mainly, I had screwed that up."

"How'd you break away from Hyde-Smith?"

"I sold my engagement ring. Ambassador Torres's personal secretary helped me find a jewelry dealer who would give me a fair price. I used the money to move out. I was fired the next day for my—" her jaw worked "—unsuitable conduct. And still, when Gerald found out I'd left, he was angry."

Her gaze turned inward, making Tyler want to tear the other man's limbs from his body. He could see in her expression just what form that anger had taken.

She moistened her lips and cleared her throat. "After that, I went to the hospital, so there were records of his behavior. And I threatened to go the media if he continued to stalk me. Apparently his self-preservation outweighed his possessiveness, and he let me go. But it was already too late for my job. I had no money...I'd had to use it for the medical expenses."

"You didn't come back here."

"My mother made it clear that I wasn't welcome. I'd failed, you see. I'd had the opportunity to have a rich and important husband, and I blew it."

"You never told them what he was really like."

"It wouldn't have mattered, Tyler," Marisa said tiredly. "She would never have believed that someone like Gerald could be so...twisted. And while Papa is very traditional, he leaves everything but the farm to my mother. Mama is… How can I explain her? Inflexible. And the truth of the matter was that I couldn't wait to get out of Mezcaya.'' She blinked and looked away, and a slow tear crept down her cheek. ''I just didn't expect the cost to be so high.''

Tyler sighed and did the only thing he could do. He pulled her into his arms and held her against his chest with one arm, and the baby with the other. He didn't want her going into *la Fortuna,* but he was damned if he knew how to prevent it.

Marisa's arms slid around his waist.

It was comfortable and tormenting all in one, he decided. ''How'd you get roped into this mission, then?''

She sighed a little. ''When Ambassador Torres notified me that he knew of a job I could help with, I jumped at the opportunity. He was retiring right about the time I left Gerald, you see. But he'd learned about me selling my ring and some of the reason why, and though his influence was limited, he said my assistance on your mission would definitely get me back in.''

''And that's all you want?''

She hesitated for a moment. ''Yes.''

Then Nicholas plopped his hands on Marisa's head and bobbled forward, kissing her, and the bubble of tension that had formed around them was broken.

Marisa let out a long breath and smiled at the child, running her fingers down the boy's cheek. "Nicholas looks just like Luis did."

"Luis?"

"My brother. The one who died from snakebite. Had he lived, he'd be twenty-three now."

"You didn't say that it was your brother who died."

"He was just a sweet little boy."

"I'm sorry."

"We all were."

He couldn't stand the sad memories in her eyes. "And Diego is what? Twenty, twenty-one?"

"Twenty-two. His wife, Teresa, is my age. Diego and Nicholas are staying with my parents until she returns from a trip to California. Usually they live with her parents in the village. Then there is Manuel and his wife, Sara. She's pregnant with their first baby."

"And Inez. What about Lydia? The little blond girl who was on your lap the day I came to. I've seen her several times since then."

Marisa's expression closed. "Lydia is Franco's. He's gone now." She stepped back and smiled, but there was no real humor in it. "My father has cousins who live in the village and work the fields with him when they can. That's why there always seems to be a steady stream of people coming and going.

And that's my family history, such as it is. What about you?''

He started walking. ''What about me?''

''Oh, Murdoch, please. Don't act dense, it doesn't become you.''

''I don't know who my dad was, and my mother got tired of that particular job early on. She preferred the bright lights of the city to parent-teacher conferences and took off.''

''And?''

''And nothing. That's it.''

She tsked. ''Murdoch—''

''Diego said there is somebody in the village with a truck they might sell.''

Her stomach tightened.

''I want to leave tomorrow.''

''How did I know you were going to say that?''

''I'm predictable, remember?''

Nine

Marisa may have believed that her family welcomed her back only because of him, but that night said differently.

It was as if, from the moment Marisa broke the news to her *abuela* that they were leaving the next day to continue their "vacation," the entire family—extended and otherwise—threw themselves into one huge spontaneous celebration to wish them well.

Marisa had finally gotten him aside to explain that it was more a celebration of their "marriage" than anything else. "We'll have great food at least."

And they did. Marisa's grandmother outdid herself. Tyler didn't think he'd ever eaten so much in his life. There'd been plenty of barbecues and parties back home in Mission Creek, but there had been none quite like what he experienced that night.

If there was one thing he could say about the Rodriguez clan, it was that they definitely knew how to party.

He just wished his "wife" were able to enjoy it a little more. She'd picked at her meal, and her smile was strained. Every time Belicia approached Marisa, she grew a little more pale, until he couldn't stand another minute of it. He leaned over to Inez and whispered in her ear, knowing that the teenager would quickly spread the gossip that her brother-in-law was taking his wife away from the crowds because he couldn't keep his hands off her.

Then he turned to Marisa and grabbed her hand. "Let's go."

She looked up at him, surprised. "Where?"

"Anywhere away from here." He tugged, and with a little shrug, she followed him. By some unspoken agreement, they headed up to the road they'd taken earlier that day. The more distance they put between themselves and the revelry that wasn't dimmed one bit by their departure, the more Marisa's tension eased until she no longer seemed to vibrate from it.

"Better?" he finally asked, when they were well away from the music and laughter and voices.

She nodded. "Yes. How did you know?"

Nobody else had seemed to notice Marisa's increasingly obvious discomfort. "Wild guess."

She tucked her hand in his arm and pressed her forehead to his shoulder. "Right. How is it that a decent guy lurks inside you, Murdoch?"

"Damn if I know."

At that, she chuckled. Then sighed. "Look at the

stars, Tyler. They're so clear and close here. It's always been like that.''

"And you still wanted to get away.''

"Yes. I did. And I guess, maybe, I'm finally getting beyond the need to apologize for that.''

"Good.''

"Is everything so cut and dried for you?''

"Me?'' He liked the feel of her arm in his, and when she started to move away, he stopped her from doing so. "I've got friends and I've got my career. Don't need much else.''

"And of course you don't need love,'' she commented dryly. "That would be too much for the guy who doesn't trust women.''

"I've got enough buddies biting the love-bullet lately, thanks.''

"You're such a romantic, Murdoch.''

"What? I like their women okay. Josie and Ellen. They're the ones who've made mincemeat of Flynt and Spence's bachelorhood. Next thing I know they'll be messing with our Sunday round of golf, too.''

Her laughter was soft. "You're having me on, now.''

Having her had been on his mind way too much lately. And he suddenly wondered about the wisdom of getting her away from her family for a while.

She veered from the road, and silent now, he followed her up the steep path. She didn't stop until they came out on an outcropping of rocks that overlooked a small valley. In the distance he could see the moonlight shining on water.

"That's the waterfall over there," she told him. "You can't quite see anything but the river below it from here, though. I used to come here when I was a child. I always loved the view. It's so…open here. More so than anywhere else around here, anyway."

"And you would dream about a life somewhere other than here."

Marisa closed her eyes. "Yes," she admitted softly. He moved up onto the grass beside her and sat. She felt that hollow feeling deep inside her and knew it had nothing whatsoever to do with not eating much at dinner. It was hunger of an entirely different sort.

"I wanted out, too," he said after a moment. "After my mom skipped, I ended up in foster homes until I graduated from high school. After that, getting into VMI was like a…I don't know. A reprieve from hell. The service suited me. It became my family."

Marisa tucked her knees beneath her long skirt. She couldn't help it. She reached over and touched his hand. She knew he was thinking about his friends, and about Westin. "I'm sorry things haven't gone as well here as you'd hoped." But when she would have removed her hand, he turned his over, catching her fingers in his.

Her breath stalled in her throat. It was dark, and there on her small patch of land where she'd spent so many nights dreaming of far-off places, it seemed far too intimate.

"You saved my life." His thumb brushed, back and forth, over her palm, scrambling her thoughts.

"Returning the favor," she managed.

His thumb moved up, grazed the sensitive flesh of her inner wrist. She swallowed. Her fingers curled.

"I don't want you going with me into *la Fortuna.*"

The fog of desire warred with the sharp pain his words caused. "Still, after everything, you can say that." She pulled at her wrist, but he held on fast.

"You've been through enough without adding a jaunt like this that may or may not end well."

"That's my decision, Tyler. Not yours. I can take care of myself."

"Can you? I can't be worrying about you when I've got Westin to deal with."

"I'm not asking you to worry about me."

"Dammit, Marisa, that's just it. I can't help it where you're concerned."

She swallowed. "If you'd said that two weeks ago, I'd never have trusted a word of it."

"And now?"

"Now I do."

"Good." Satisfaction rolled through Tyler. "There's not much I can do about your family, I know. But I'm not without my own share of influence. I'll make sure the ambassador knows all that you've done. You'll never have to waitress and do oddball translating jobs again. Not unless you want to. And if it doesn't work out with the Embassy for some reason, I've got other connections."

She was staring at him as if he'd lost his mind. "What are you talking about?"

"I'm talking about getting things turned around for you."

"You're talking about doing things that I am perfectly capable of doing myself! Tyler, I don't need you to save me. What I need is for you to let me do what I'm here to do!"

"What? Go into *la Fortuna* and get yourself killed?"

"That is ridiculous! It's more likely that you'd get yourself killed, and you darned well know it."

"I don't want to chance you getting hurt." He couldn't get past it. That was all there was to it.

"Murdoch—"

He caught her hand. "Marisa, think about it. I'll make sure the powers-that-be know how much you helped. You'll have your career back."

"You need me."

"More than that I need you to be safe."

"Why? We've come this far, surely—"

"You know why."

Her lips parted and she stared at his hand, wrapped warm and strong around her wrist. The moon shone down, clear and white. Her heartbeat tripped unevenly as that strong, excruciatingly masculine hand slid up her forearm, grazed over her elbow and curled gently around her upper arm. Her nipples tightened against the cool cotton of her dress.

"I won't betray you like Sonya did," she whispered.

"I know." His thumb continued taunting her senses as it slowly moved along her arm, brushing the outer curve of her breast. "You want to go around in circles the rest of the night?"

Her throat tightened. "No."

His head lowered until she felt the warmth of his breath on her temple. "What do you want?"

Her eyelids felt weighted. It was a good thing she was sitting, because she felt decidedly lightheaded. "Tyler," she breathed. "Please, I…"

"Just say it, Marisa." His low murmur sent shivers dancing down her back, almost as if he'd drawn his fingertips down her spine. "I won't take what you don't offer."

"I know." Forming the words seemed ridiculously difficult. He wasn't Gerald. He'd never stoop to force. He'd never need to.

After a moment, he stood, and the movement was easy and full of caged energy, proving more than anything that he was physically ready to finish the mission to save Westin whether or not the cut on his shoulder was fully healed. His fingers circled her wrists and he drew her to her feet. The flowing folds of the skirt swished around her calves, sounding loud in the still night.

His chest lifted in a long breath that he exhaled slowly. "Okay." He pressed a kiss to her forehead. "You're right. This is a bad idea." He turned to go.

As she watched him walk away, her voice finally broke free. "Tyler."

She saw his shoulders stiffen. She thought he would keep going, but he didn't. He turned to look at her. His jaw was so tight, his eyes so shadowed, that she wanted to weep for all the loss and lack she knew he'd endured in his life.

She moistened her lips, and slowly pulled her arms free of the ruffled bodice.

He went utterly still.

She drew the dress downward, until it was at her waist, then slid the fabric farther, past her hips. It fell, unfettered, to the ground beneath her bare feet, sighing into a puddle of midnight cotton.

Tyler couldn't speak to save his soul as Marisa

stood there, naked but for the moonlight bathing her golden body in silver. The fine chain around her neck glistened.

"I *don't* think it's a bad idea," she said huskily. "Just for tonight, Tyler. Don't go."

She was so beautiful, she made him ache in ways that went beyond the physical. Every speck of common sense told him to walk away. No matter that he'd basically forced the issue, he still knew he shouldn't touch her. She deserved more than he could ever give her.

He was a soldier. Half his life was spent on the road, involved in work that the rest of the decent world couldn't even acknowledge a need for.

As if sensing the struggle inside him, Marisa stepped beyond the drift of dress and took one step, then another, toward him. "Show me how it is supposed to be, Tyler."

She continued forward, until the hair springing back from her temples brushed his chin. He could feel her breath, warm and sweet, on his collarbone.

Then she reached for his shirt. She tugged and he lowered his head, letting her pull it off. Which she did with that blend of earnestness and earthiness that never failed to arouse him.

When she began unfastening his jeans, he closed his eyes, sucking in his breath at her delicate touch.

Her fingers faltered, her sudden uncertainty nearly visible.

"No one's ever done that before," he muttered.

"Done what?"

"Undressed me."

Her lashes lowered slowly. "Not even..."

"Not even." He drew her hands back, felt them curl warmly into the waist of his jeans. "Maybe there are some things left for you to show me."

She smiled softly and finished the task. She murmured over the cut on his shoulder. She sifted her fingers through the hair on his chest. She stepped up to him, fitting her lush curves against him, catching her breath audibly when he ran his hands down her back, finally stopping to settle on the seductive flare of her hips.

Her hair streamed over his arm as he bent her back, tasting that spot on her throat where the cross carefully nestled, always guarding, always protecting. And lower. Exploring the taut, golden skin curving over her shoulders. Adoring the tight crests of her breasts, the warmth of the valley between.

A soft sound escaped her lips as he spread his shirt on the thick grass and lowered her onto it. Her arms lifted, silently beckoning when he stopped, nearly undone by the sight of her beneath him.

Wanton. Soft. Innocent. Strong. She was all those

things, and so many more. Whether he liked it or not, she'd gotten lodged under his skin.

Then she curled her hands around his neck, pulling his head down to hers. She pressed her lips to his. Murmured his name. Twined one leg around his, and wordlessly offered all that she had to give.

Tyler took. And, heaven help him, as he sank deep into her body and heard her cry of pleasure, he knew that with her *everything* was just as it was supposed to be.

Ten

He'd left without her.

The old Jeep that he'd bought in the village was no longer parked outside the house when Marisa awakened, alone, the next morning. She'd immediately gone to the window, only to confirm what her heart already knew.

He'd gone to *Fortaleza de la Fortuna* without her.

Only a few days ago and she would have taken it as the ultimate proof of his distrust. Now Marisa knew better. He believed it was the only way to protect her from harm.

Clutching the thin sheet to her body, she turned and looked at the bed. They'd walked back several hours before dawn only to fall into that bed there and make love again.

Even now her cheeks warmed at the things they'd done. The time and the care with which they'd silently explored each other. Seeking out and finding every delicious spot, tarrying in the most decadent of ways...

She yanked back her hair from her eyes and

forced the memory back. It wouldn't go far. Her nerve endings still hummed, and her body ached in ways that made her skin heat to think about.

But she had to think about practical matters now. The most important of which was Tyler and the likelihood of him gaining access to *la Fortuna* without her.

He wasn't the only one who had business there.

She hurriedly cleaned up and dressed in clothes she pinched from Inez. Then she went and found her grandmother, and hugged the old woman goodbye.

"You are a good girl," her grandmother said, patting Marisa's cheek just as she'd done when Marisa was a young girl, leaving a smudge of flour from the bread she'd been kneading. "Your man, he is a fine one. Not like that other." Her lip curled in disgust. "Belicia was always taken too much with fanciness, with the glossy stuff she would read in the magazines. She wanted you to have what she did not. And her pride kept her from seeing that you were right to be rid of that man."

"*Abuela,* the only reason she welcomed me back is because of Tyler. She thinks he is a rich American because he owned the plane we flew down here. And a rich American, in her mind, is even better than a rich Brit."

Her grandmother waved that away with a floury hand. "It is good you concern yourself with your parents' wishes for you. But not good if it blinds you to your own happiness."

"*Abuela—*"

"I see the way you look at him, *niña.* And the way he looks at you. Yet he drives away this morning before the sun."

Marisa paused. How *did* Tyler look at her? "I'm going after him."

"On your *vacation,*" her grandmother said the word disbelievingly.

Marisa chewed her lip, nodded.

The old woman clucked and shook her grayed head. "You never were good at untruths, Marisa. But go. Go after your man."

"*Abuela,* he's not— I mean, Tyler and I—"

"Shush. You love him, yes?"

Her lips parted, a denial forming. But the words wouldn't emerge.

Her grandmother smiled slightly. "You tell Franco when you see him that his daughter needs her father."

Shock coursed through her. "*Abuela,* why would you think—"

"This old woman's eyes still see plenty, *niña.* You learned about Franco's fool's chase and thought to make amends through him. Yes?"

Marisa leaned back against the table. "I…yes."

The old woman shook her head, disgusted. "It is

my stubborn Belicia who needs to make amends. First she blames you for saving yourself from that idiot, then she not keep Franco from his own course of idiocy. But Belicia too old to change. But you, *niña,* you are young. It is easier for you to forgive. Maybe next time you won't let so many months go before you do.''

Then she flopped the bread around on the board and attacked it with relish, looking as if she could easily be kneading bread even twenty years from now. But Marisa knew better. Her grandmother wouldn't be around forever. And Marisa didn't know what would transpire in the next few days. She believed Tyler would succeed. Of that she had no doubts.

She only prayed that it wasn't too late for Franco. And once Tyler knew that she did have an ulterior motive for getting into *la Fortuna,* he'd probably never trust her again.

It was an unbearable thought. She leaned down and kissed her grandmother, then quickly left before the old woman could divine even more of Marisa's thoughts.

She "borrowed" Diego's truck as he'd gone out already with their father, salving her conscience with the promise that somehow she'd make sure it was returned to him. And then she drove, as fast as the rough roads and the old truck would allow, after

Tyler while her grandmother's words rang in her ears.

You love him, yes?

Tyler didn't think he'd ever been the focus of quite so many suspicious people at one time. And he'd been in plenty of close fixes before.

The background information they'd gathered had said most of the people who worked at *la Fortuna* passed through this cantina at one time or another. But he hadn't even been able to mention the compound before the closemouthed locals sitting around the tables in the open-air cantina were giving him the evil eye.

So he ordered a tequila, found a chair at an unoccupied table and sat down. He ignored the stares, the curiosity and the hostility, and after a long moment, he ceased being the center of attention as conversations picked up again.

Thanks to the tutoring that Marisa had given him while he'd been recuperating, he even managed to recognize some of the words he overhead. But mostly, he knew, they could be plotting fifty ways to skin him alive and he wouldn't have known it.

He tossed back the shot, and ordered another, which he didn't really intend to drink. But slouching over it gave him an opportunity to get a lay of the land.

There was a gray-haired woman across the cantina talking agitatedly to the bartender. Her voice kept rising despite the shushing the man gave her.

A trio of young men climbed out of a fire-engine-red pickup that could just as easily have been right back home in Mission Creek. In the truck bed, Tyler could see landscaping equipment. Lots of it. There was a possibility, he thought.

The woman was yelling now, making it impossible for him to hear anything at all from the trio who'd joined another group at a long table. The bartender waved his hand at her as he placed pitchers of beer on the table for the new arrivals.

And then the cantina went silent again.

His neck prickled, even before he looked over and saw who'd done the silencing this time. Marisa. Wearing cutoff jeans and a red shirt tied at her midriff.

She spotted him. He barely had time to put his chair back on all fours before she dashed over to him and launched herself into his arms, noisily chattering away in Mezcayan as she pressed kisses to his cheeks.

He started to push her away, but she wound her arms tighter around his neck. "I'll forgive you later for this," she murmured in his ear, then hopped off his lap and headed over to the bar, managing to look sexy and dejected, all at once.

Tyler reached for his drink and watched as Marisa somehow managed to engage half the place in conversation without earning herself one single look of suspicion. Wearing a pout the size of Texas, she returned to his table and sat down on his lap, bold as you please.

"What the hell are you doing?" His voice was a whisper in her ear.

She tossed back her hair and toyed with her bottle of beer. "We're arguing, husband-mine," she murmured. "And that woman over there, she's sympathetic, because she's arguing with her husband, too."

Tyler watched the bartender deliver another round to the long table. "She's not sitting on her husband's lap."

Marisa looked at him, her eyes full of sharp humor. "Is it bothering you?"

He clamped his hands over her wriggling hips. "Dammit, Marisa, this isn't a joke."

She hopped up again and burst into tears.

He blinked. "Marisa—"

But she'd already thrown herself into the gray-haired woman's arms, sobbing dramatically. The woman gave him a censorious glare that transcended language.

He decided maybe he should drink his tequila, after all. The woman clucked and murmured to Marisa as they huddled together. If nothing else, Tyler thought with disbelief, the bartender had gotten a reprieve from the woman's haranguing.

He had begun to think he'd have to do something, anything, to get Marisa out of there and come up with an alternate plan to get into *la Fortuna,* when she suddenly returned to his table, all smiles. She held out her hand, beckoning him. Wondering what rabbit hole he'd fallen down, he went with her.

Ten minutes later, they were following the gray-haired woman from the cantina through an iron gate situated in an enormous stone wall.

They were in. *Fortaleza de la Fortuna.* Slick as you please.

It was too damn easy, Tyler thought suspiciously. He half expected to hear a gun being cocked on them at any moment. But nobody shouted at them. No body pointed. No alarms rang and no dogs charged after them.

The only sign of Marisa's nervousness, however, was in the tight clasp of her hand on his as they followed the woman up to an imposing house.

Hell, Tyler thought as he looked up at the pillared thing, it was a damn mansion. They went in through the back, into a kitchen that was positively crawling with activity. Marisa chattered with the woman as if they were long-lost friends, and Tyler found himself relegated to a chair in a corner of the busy room.

It looked to him as if they were cooking to feed an army.

But then, considering the breadth of El Jefe's terrorism, maybe it was an army.

Then Marisa came back to him and led him outside, where there was nearly as much activity going on as in the kitchen.

"Graciela says you can work in the gardens today." Her words were low, hurried. "There is some sort of big dinner tomorrow night with all the generals. Key people, I guess. It was last minute, and that's why she was so upset at the cantina. She's in charge of the kitchen staff and they're not at all prepared."

"And just like that she lets us in here? Even though I'm not Mezcayan."

Marisa's eyes didn't meet his. "She thinks I'm a chef, but you want us to go back to the States 'cause you can't seem to find work here, and I don't want to leave Mezcaya. What can I say? She probably thinks she's saving a marriage or something, plus she's got more help for tomorrow night. She said there are quarters for the staff here. She'll make arrangements. She also said for you to go see Henry and tell him her name. He's working in the rose gardens right now. He's in charge of the gardeners."

Tyler didn't care what excuse Marisa used. They

were in. And nobody had given them a second glance.

It seemed that she was more than capable of fending for herself. For now. "Can you cook?"

"Can you garden?" She leaned up to him, pressed a kiss to his cheek and darted back into the kitchen.

Tyler slowly turned in a circle. Inside the stone walls, the roads were paved, the grounds immaculately kept. The buildings, aside from the mansion, were all blinding white stucco, with red-tiled roofs. Statuary dotted the lush green lawns. It had a hideous, arrogant beauty to it, he thought, knowing the sordid truth behind the resources that supported such lavishness.

And somewhere amongst the perfect buildings, the perfect hedges, the perfect garden paths, Lieutenant Colonel Phillip Westin was being held prisoner.

But not for much longer, Tyler promised silently.

"How an Americano like you get yourself a girl like that?"

The voice came from behind him, and Tyler turned to see a young man leaning against the wall, arms folded atop a shovel.

"I thought nobody here spoke English."

The man's lip curled in disgust. "Maybe some don't speak it, but most understand it. What you doing with the girl?"

Tyler's hands stayed at his side. "She's mine."

"You sure about that?"

"Anybody makes the mistake of trespassing, they'll find out," he said flatly. "I don't share."

The other man nodded thoughtfully, but his eyes were narrowed. "Watch yourself here. Watch her." Then he swung the shovel, propping the long handle on his shoulder as he wandered off.

Tyler watched the man head over a small, lush hill. He wasn't sure what kind of warning he'd just received.

He looked back at the open door of the kitchen and caught sight of Marisa carrying a burlap sack of potatoes. She glanced up and saw him. She smiled faintly before she walked out of sight.

Yeah, he thought. He'd be watching out for her, all right.

And for once, he actually believed that someone other than his buddies back in Mission Creek would be watching out for him.

Just after noon Tyler learned that nearly the entire population of *la Fortuna* shut down for siesta. It was such a traditional thing, he was surprised by it. Nevertheless, when Marisa found him, and they followed a teenaged boy to the quarters they'd been assigned, he was glad for the break.

The daypack that he'd brought with him had been

thoroughly searched by a guard when he'd found Henry in the rose garden. The ''pager'' had earned him a superior laugh from the guard who'd done the search and for a minute, Tyler had thought it might be confiscated. He'd hoped not, but he'd been prepared for that eventuality. He was closer to Westin than anybody had been able to get so far. Whether he had the disguised transmitter to fall back on or not didn't matter to him, though it would make things considerably easier in the end if he could use it.

But the guard had dismissed the device as useless down here in *la Fortuna* and tossed it into the pack. The switchblade that Tyler had, however, was taken. As was the wallet containing Tyler's fake ID and five hundred American dollars.

The guard had stared at him, challenge in his hard eyes, as he'd returned the pack to him. Tyler had waited until the guard went on his way and he was arm deep in rose bushes to permit a brief, satisfied smile.

Now, in the small cell of a room, Tyler held his fingers to Marisa's lips before he checked the room for surveillance devices. He took his time and made sure he was thorough. But there was none. Not a single one.

Which didn't mean that he relaxed, exactly. He pulled Marisa into his arms and pressed his mouth close to her ear. "Watch what you say," he murmured. "The powers that be probably figure the grunts around here don't need to be surveilled, but you never know. I might have missed something."

Marisa was practically vibrating with excitement. "I don't think any of the servants' quarters are watched. You wouldn't believe the things they talked about in the kitchen. If they were worried about being overheard, I'm sure they wouldn't have been so free with their comments."

"What kind of things?" He still didn't let Marisa out of his arms.

Not that she seemed in any hurry to go, either. "Graciela is the head chef, right? She's a sister of one of the generals. That's how she got such a position of authority. But even she doesn't let that keep her from gossiping."

"About what?"

"Oh, how much money it takes to run this place. The power struggle between the top generals. Who is sleeping with whom."

He blew out an impatient breath. "I don't give a damn about that stuff."

Marisa caught his earlobe gently between her teeth and he felt her smile against him. "Are you sure?"

His hands slid over her waist. "Witch. Stop distracting me. Anything else they talk about?"

"No. Some guy they called Mendez came in and that was pretty much the end of the gossip. He took a liking to me, though, I could tell."

"What do you mean?"

She shrugged. "Just the look he gave me. Considering the way everyone went quiet, he must have some measure of authority."

"Stay away from him."

"Tyler, I can't learn anything if I don't take advantage of the opportunities that present themselves. That's one of the reasons why I'm here, for heaven's sake."

"You got me into this place. That's all I needed you to do. Don't put yourself in more danger, Marisa. I mean it."

She fingered his collar. "Don't you want to know about the dinner tomorrow night?"

He sighed and grabbed her fingers. "You're gonna be the death of me. What about it?"

"It's something big. All the key people of El Jefe will be there. Something that hasn't occurred, I guess, in a year or so. It's got all the staff in a tizzy."

"Any talk about prisoners?"

She shook her head, her eyes serious. "No. I'm sorry, Tyler."

"He's gotta be here somewhere. Luke said something about a cave. El Jefe's been holding Westin over our heads for too long for them to have just disposed of him.''

She winced. ''Makes him sound like some piece of trash.''

''El Jefe figured they had a bargaining chip when they captured him,'' Tyler explained quietly. ''Only they're learning we don't make deals with terrorists. There are other methods.''

''Like sending you down here.''

''I asked for the assignment.''

''Because of what he's done for you in the past.''

''I owe him.''

''And loyalty means a lot to you,'' she concluded. She slipped out of his arms and prowled the narrow confines of the room. It contained only a small bed, a chest of drawers and a lamp. Not many places to hide a bug. Not much to make him forget about the bed.

He watched her toy with the small cross at her neck, and wondered what was making her so nervous. ''Aside from this Mendez guy, the guards all know you're mine,'' he said, hazarding a guess.

She looked at him, her expression startled. Then it cleared. ''I know what the dangers are here only too well, Tyler. I'm not worried about my safety, if that's what you mean. I know you'll take care of that.''

He finally sat on the foot of the bed. The mattress

was way too soft. If they slept on it together, they'd both roll toward the center. He shut off the thought. "Yeah, that's what I mean." What else? They'd been forced to depend on each other, they'd worked together, they'd slept together. But that was it. Wasn't it?

Wasn't it?

She started pacing again, telling him easily enough that her supposed married status was not what had her wound up. "If he is a bargaining piece, they'd be foolish to do something to him. What do they want in return?"

He shook his head. "I don't know. Maybe it's just payback." He grabbed her hand and pulled her down to his lap. "El Jefe's drug money was making inroads into Mission Creek a while back. Westin was helping to put a stop to it. At the source, down here. I tell you, Marisa, once I find him, I'd like to blow this entire place to hell."

She looked startled. "You can't. There are people here, people I—"

"I know. I didn't say I'd do it, I said I'd *like* to do it."

"Tyler, there's something I should—" A pounding at the door accompanied by a shout startled her into silence. She jumped off his lap, as if she'd been caught with her hand in the cookie jar. "I've got to go." She reached for the doorknob.

"Marisa."

"Hmm?"

He thought about the guy who'd given him the warning. "Be careful. Stay with the other women. Don't let anyone get you alone. Especially that Mendez guy."

She tilted her head, her lips parting. Then she smiled a little. "You be careful, too. I, um, Graciela said all the servants eat together after the main meal has been served."

"Then I guess you'd better save me a seat."

Her eyes flickered to the bed as color rose in her cheeks. "I will. Tyler, this is almost over, right?"

"Soon as we get Westin out."

She moistened her lips and looked about to say something. But she didn't. She just darted back to him and pressed a fierce kiss to his lips before hurrying out the door.

Eleven

"Get your hands off my wife."

At the furiously cold voice, Marisa nearly sagged with relief. She'd managed to wedge her arm between herself and Mendez, but had begun to despair of being able to avoid the man's disgusting advances.

"I said, get your hands off her."

Marisa shrank back as Tyler bodily pulled the beefy guard away from her. She'd seen the amount of wine the man had tossed back hours earlier at dinner, and could hardly believe he was still standing, much less taking a foolhardy swing at Tyler, who easily dodged it.

But when Mendez turned like an enraged bull and plowed into Tyler, slamming him back against the big, commercial freezer against the wall, Marisa cried out. She ran over and grabbed him from behind.

"Dammit, Marisa," Tyler gritted as he deflected Mendez's wild punches. "Get away from here before you get hurt."

"She's a wildcat." Mendez whirled around, with Marisa clinging to his beefy back like an annoying insect. "Takes two men to satisfy her." He laughed.

Marisa's skin crawled. She tightened her arm around the man's neck. He thumped her, hard, against the wall, and all the breath left her body. Her arms loosened, and she gasped for air.

And then the man suddenly hit the floor.

Marisa stared, dismayed, at Tyler who was standing over the unconscious guard. Her knees started to buckle and she slid down the wall. She drew in one painful breath after another as Tyler raked his fingers through his hair and stared back.

"So much for staying inconspicuous," he said after a moment. "Are you all right?"

She nodded. She felt as if she'd been hit by a truck, but she'd live. "Tyler, I didn't encourage him. He—"

"I know. You don't have to explain."

Her lips parted, her heart skidding. "You believe me."

"Yes. Here, take my hands. Can you stand? Are you hurt anywhere?"

She shook her head, letting him pull her to her feet. She gently touched his shoulder. He looked unnaturally pale. "He didn't hurt *you?*"

"You've got no business being involved in this, Marisa."

"Maybe I'm watching your back. Now, did he hurt your shoulder or not?"

He smiled faintly. "I'm tougher than I look."

Her smile felt shaky. He *was* tough. But beneath that toughness, his heart was as vulnerable as anyone else's, though she knew he'd deny it until his last breath. She looked down at the man sprawled on the floor. "What do we do with him?"

A voice came from the doorway.

"Put him where he can't be found until you get the hell out of here."

Marisa turned in the direction of the voice. "Franco!"

His hair was longer than it used to be, and his shoulders were broader. He was no longer a young man left alone with a baby and a broken heart. He was a man.

Tyler had gone still beside her. "Franco?" His voice was soft, smooth. "Your brother Franco?"

Marisa felt the world closing in on her. Tyler's expression was hard. Franco's was no better. She moistened her lips. She wanted her brother to stop his madness, but she wanted Tyler to find Phillip Westin, too. "Yes," she whispered.

Only Tyler had moved away from her to stand by the unconscious Mendez. "I don't suppose this one told you where the cave was while he was pawing you?"

"No." And she felt like a fool because of it. The only reason she'd let Mendez corner her in the deserted kitchen at this late hour was because she'd believed that she could elicit information from the man.

So much for that.

"Of course, with a brother who's part of El Jefe, you're not likely to tell me, anyway," Tyler continued. "No wonder Graciela let us in here like you were a long lost friend. You probably tossed around your brother's name."

"Tyler, Franco's not—"

"What was the point of coming this far, Marisa? Why not just stick the knife in right from the start? Is there some particular thrill you get from doing it after you get me to fall for you?"

Her knees went weak. "Tyler, I promise you—"

"Spare me." His lips twisted as he looked over at Franco, his big body braced for battle. "Well? You gonna issue more obscure warnings or do what you came here to do? Because you're gonna have to take me out to stop me from getting to Westin."

Franco's dark gaze bore into his before sliding to Marisa. He entered the big kitchen and quietly swung the door shut, flicking the lock.

Tyler immediately scoped out other exits.

"You need to leave here, Marisa," Franco said flatly. "Soon. I don't know who or what Westin is, and I don't care. But the generals are gathering tomorrow night, and I'm finally going to avenge Jennifer."

Tyler paused. The tension between Marisa and Franco was thick, tangible. Marisa cast him a beseeching look that he couldn't begin to interpret before she walked over to Franco, catching his hands in hers.

"Getting yourself killed won't bring back Jennifer, Franco. Lydia needs you."

Franco shrugged off her hands. He walked around the big island in the center of the room, watching Tyler warily. He crouched down beside Mendez, studying the man. "How did you even learn I was here? Nobody knew."

"Valencia knew."

"Valencia always did talk too much."

Tyler raked back his hair. "Somebody want to fill me in here?"

Franco looked up at him. "There's butcher twine in the cupboard behind you. Get it."

"You think twine is gonna hold me?"

"Oh, Tyler, stop it. Franco isn't part of El Jefe." Marisa went to the cupboard herself and yanked it open, pulling out a thick spool. She handed it to her brother, who used it to secure Mendez's arms behind his back.

Franco looked up at Tyler. "Help me pull him

into the closet there. With luck, he won't be discovered until breakfast preparations begin.''

Tyler exhaled impatiently. "I'm not doing one bloody thing until I get an explanation.''

"Will you believe it, anyway?'' Marisa whispered. Her eyes glistened. "I should have told you, Tyler, I know that. But Franco is just as much a victim as Westin.''

Tyler glanced down at her brother. Franco had tired of waiting for assistance and was slowly dragging Mendez's bulk toward the closet. "Right.''

Marisa went over to help her brother. "We're making too much noise. What if someone hears and comes looking?''

Franco reached behind him.

Tyler braced himself, ready for anything. But the other man merely held up the nine millimeter with his fingers. He set it on the counter and continued dragging Mendez. "Use that.''

Tyler grabbed the weapon and checked the clip. It was fully loaded. He tucked it in the small of his back. Marisa *wasn't* Sonya, he reminded himself. She was nothing like that witch. He exhaled and joined Franco, brushing Marisa aside. In seconds, Mendez was safely locked in the closet. "Who the hell is Jennifer?''

"Lydia's mother,'' Marisa said softly, watching both men. Her heart ached for her brother. It ached for Tyler, for the words that he'd spoken in anger about falling for her. If it were true, she feared he'd never forgive her for keeping silent about Franco.

"We were to be married," Franco said. "As soon as she finished her assignment from the magazine."

Jennifer. It clicked and Tyler groaned a little. "Jennifer Tate." His gaze pinned Marisa and she knew he was remembering the conversation they'd had before the plane crash. "The reporter."

"She did travel features for a London news magazine," Franco corrected. "We met in Cozumel where I was working. It took me weeks to get her to go out. She was a few years older than me, but I convinced her." His lips curled in a maudlin smile.

"How did a travel reporter end up in this place?"

"Jennifer wanted to be an investigative reporter, and she believed an exposé of El Jefe's compound would gain her a reassignment on the magazine," Marisa explained. "Franco didn't know until she was found afterward where she'd been headed, or he'd have stopped her from coming here."

"I thought she'd gotten over the attack," Franco murmured, his expression tormented. "We all did."

Marisa nodded gently. "She'd just become pregnant with Lydia that last time I visited Mezcaya before going to London."

"We planned to marry," Franco murmured. "But

she kept putting off the wedding, saying after the baby came. But she—''

Tyler knew what the young woman had done. ''And what are you planning to do? Destroy all the generals when they're together sitting around the table tomorrow night? Franco, you're one man. You can't fight them all.''

''And what is it *you* are doing here?''

Tyler grimaced. He *was* prepared to take on however many as he had to in order to get Westin out of there. But he had at least ten years experience on Franco. He pulled out a stool and sat on it, drumming his fingers on the countertop. ''We can't wait until tomorrow night. Mendez will be missed long before then.'' He looked at Franco. ''All the servants are in their quarters for the night,'' he said, looking pointedly at Marisa, who had *not* been in their quarters when she'd said she would be, which was why he'd come looking for her. ''So it may be a good time. The guards are pretty minimal, too, from what I could tell.'' He looked at Franco. ''I don't suppose you know anything about a cave around here, do you? I know there's a series of caverns in Guatemala, and I suppose there are more like it here.''

''Caves?'' Franco's expression suddenly cleared, and he grinned broadly. ''*Sí*. The Cave. That's what they call the dungeon. There's no sunlight down there.''

"A dungeon," Tyler repeated with disbelief.

"There are statues of Zeus and Apollo in the gardens," Marisa said hurriedly. "El Jefe's known for its excesses. Why not a dungeon, too?"

"All right," Tyler said. He stood and held out his hand to Marisa. She blinked, then took it, curling her fingers securely through his. "Franco, you show us to the dungeon and help me get Westin out of it, and I'll take care of dismantling their operation for you."

Franco looked as if he wanted to argue.

"Please, Franco," Marisa begged softly. "Getting yourself killed is not going to help Lydia. Hasn't she already lost enough to El Jefe? Tyler knows what he's doing, I promise you."

The young man hesitated, then sighed heavily. "The entrance to the dungeon is from the outside on the north side of the building. Two guards at the door. One at the base of the stairs. Beyond that, I don't know what you'll find."

Marisa blinked back her tears. She looked at Tyler. "Thank you."

He blew out a noisy breath and hauled her close for a hard kiss. "Thank me once we get our butts out of here."

In the end, Tyler would look back and say the rescue went surprisingly smoothly. Marisa looked at him as if he'd lost his mind when he sent her back to the room to retrieve his backpack.

By the time she met him on the north side of the darkened building, he and Franco had dealt with the guards there. Fortunately Franco had come up with something far more substantial than butcher twine to immobilize them.

While Tyler set off the transmitter, Marisa distracted the guard at the base of the narrow stairs with nothing more than a wink and a toss of her long hair. Which left Tyler wondering just how dedicated El Jefe's guards were.

He glanced up at Marisa who was helping her brother tie up the third guard while he worked the lock in the iron door. He had to admit she was a distracting sight.

"Hurry," Franco hissed. "The guards change at midnight."

Tyler quickened his efforts with the lock, using the small tools that he'd pulled from the thick plastic lining of the daypack.

At last, he heard the satisfying *click*. The door swung open and Franco directed the heavy flashlight into the depths.

He held his breath, feeling Marisa come up next to him, clasping his hand anxiously as the golden light bounced over the walls and floor.

And there, in the corner on a bare cot, sat a man,

squinting into the light. "If you're going to kill me, just be done with it," he said in a hoarse, commanding voice.

Marisa felt Tyler's shoulders sag, and knew then that no matter how much Tyler had said about Phillip Westin, he'd barely glossed the surface of what the man meant to him. She covered her mouth with her hand, blinking back tears.

"Not tonight, sir," Tyler said. "We'd just as soon skip that part if you don't mind."

Lieutenant Colonel Phillip Westin frowned. He tried to stand, but his legs were too weak. "Who is that?"

"Friends," Tyler said huskily as he strode across the dark room and simply swung his former C.O. over his shoulder in a fireman's lift and carried him up the narrow flight of stairs.

Behind him, Franco locked the guards inside the iron dungeon and then they were all racing silently for the gate. There was a guard on the opposite side, Tyler remembered from earlier that day when they'd arrived. Gritting his teeth against the renewed pain in his shoulder, he carefully lowered Westin to the ground, cursing when he saw the man had lost consciousness.

"Where's the backpack?"

Marisa held it up, and he unzipped one pocket and pulled out the pack of gum. She stared incredulously. "I carried that around so you could chew gum?"

"It packs a mean punch," he whispered dryly. "Stay with Westin. You're shielded right here by the bushes. Ricky should be here with the chopper in less than an hour."

"Where are you going?"

"Keeping my deal with Franco."

She caught his hand. "Tyler—"

"I'll be back, Marisa," he said softly. "I won't leave you."

Marisa never felt time drag so slowly as she sat there, cradling Westin's head carefully in her lap, counting off the minutes by the pounding of her heart as she waited.

She wished it were a cloudy night so that Tyler's and Franco's surreptitious movements around the buildings of the compound were not so obvious.

And just when she thought she'd go mad from waiting, she heard a shout. Her heart stopped and she shrank back into the shadows as much as the bushes would allow.

A flurry of footsteps sounded nearby, just as the sky filled with sound. Tyler grabbed Westin and Franco hauled Marisa to her feet. "Run," Tyler yelled at Marisa as he kicked open the heavy gate. The guard on the other side lifted his weapon, but

Franco grabbed it, knocking the butt of it into the man's jaw. He sank like a stone.

The last thing Marisa saw was Tyler's grimace as he lifted Westin over his shoulders again and stumbled after them.

Then the ground shook, and Marisa fell forward, crying out. Franco grabbed her, and still they ran. Ran toward the helicopter that was kicking up a blinding dust as it settled on the ground.

Twelve

"Who is this Marisa who helped you?"

Tyler rolled up the sleeves of his uniform and sat down on the chair beside Westin's hospital bed. They were in the infirmary at the British base in Belize. Westin had regained consciousness nearly immediately when given an IV. He'd been dehydrated and half-starved. But he would be fine.

"She's a linguistics expert," he finally said in answer to Westin's question. The flint-eyed man was in a hospital gown, propped against pillows, with tubes running into his arms, and still he was a commanding presence. "And she'll be back in Embassy service quicker than we can say spit."

"You had to work with her."

Tyler nodded. "She was…useful."

Westin made no comment to that. "And Ricky Mercado has been useful, as well."

Again Tyler nodded. "We never talk about Haley's death. It's…" He didn't know what word would adequately describe the tension that still existed between Ricky Mercado and the rest of his friends who'd been present the night Haley had drowned. "Easier," he finally settled on. "Everyone's been debriefed. He went to notify Luke that we got you out."

"And how *is* Luke?"

"Last I saw him, he was still in the hospital, recuperating. I guess you knew about his undercover work."

Westin didn't deny it. His sharp gaze pinned Tyler, making him feel uncomfortably like a raw recruit again. "What's on your agenda now?"

Tyler shrugged. "There's a consultation in Geneva that I was asked to participate in before I came down to Central America. It's sometime this fall, I guess. There's also a class they want me to teach out at the base at Mission Creek. But that all sounds too tame for me these days."

"And Marisa?"

He sighed. "What about her?"

Westin looked impatient. "I had nothing but time down in that hole, Tyler. You've been a hostage, you know what I mean. A man does a lot of thinking in circumstances like those. You worked with this woman. You haven't done that in years."

"I told you, she was helpful."

"She means something to you."

"Sir—"

Westin lifted a hand. "Hear me out, son. Then

you go do whatever the hell it is you want to do.''
His lips twisted wryly. ''You will anyway. You're a
lot like me, Tyler. That isn't necessarily a compliment. I let myself focus too hard on my career once.
And because of it, I walked away from the one
woman who ever meant anything to me.''

He shifted, uncomfortable. ''Sir, it's none of
my—''

''Shut up, Tyler, and listen to me.''

Tyler shut up.

''I knew Patrice in college. She wanted to get
married, but I wanted the rest of the world. I just
couldn't see a compromise between our two lives,
so I walked away. And regretted it ever since.''

''Sir—''

''I kept up with her.'' Westin's hard blue gaze
was turned inward. ''From a distance. She never
knew about it. I knew when she got married. When
she had her first child. And her second and her third.
It's a hard thing, Tyler, watching the woman you
love live a full and complete life without you.''

''Sir—''

''That's all I've got to say, son. You just think
about it some before you go tearing off to fight your
next injustice.'' Then Westin closed his eyes, effectively dismissing Tyler, never giving him an opportunity to say that he had no intentions of letting Ma-

risa go. He just didn't know whether she'd have any intention of staying.

"Ma'am, this fax came for you this afternoon. I also believe these are yours."

Marisa turned at the clipped British accent. The young, clean-cut soldier held out a sheet of white paper and a small manila envelope. She took them from him. "Thank you."

He nodded once and disappeared, his hard shoes clicking on the tiled corridor.

They'd been at the British base in Belize for nearly a day, yet Marisa had seen neither Tyler nor Westin since their chopper had carried them all to safety. It was almost as if she'd ceased to exist.

Except that she'd just spent several hours sitting in this cold, barren office, being debriefed by men she'd never before seen.

She looked out the window again. The helicopter that Tyler had summoned still sat out on the square of concrete. She didn't know why the sight of it comforted her. Tyler could leave, if he hadn't already, by any kind of means.

She sat down at the table, and with nothing else to do, tore open the envelope. All the identification that Tyler had taken from her that day at the airfield slid out in a pile on top of the fax. She squared them all and slid them into the pocket of the khaki shirt-dress she'd been loaned.

She read through the fax from Ambassador Torres and sighed a little. He'd kept his word. The new ambassador would appoint her to his staff within a week.

She moved the fax to the center of the table and stared at it for a long while, then turned with a start when she heard a noise outside the window.

The helicopter was taking off.

She left the office at a run, turning corridor after corridor, finally bursting through the metal doors that led out to the field. But all she could see was the bottom of the chopper as it flew away.

Her feet carried her out to the spot where it had sat all day and she watched through a blur of tears until it flew from sight.

He'd left.

It didn't matter whether Tyler had fallen for her or not. He would never forgive her for keeping the truth about Franco from him. She'd gotten just what she deserved.

"Marisa."

And now she was hearing Tyler's voice on the breeze. She chewed at her lip. He'd told her she was strong, yet just then she felt like collapsing.

"Marisa."

She dashed away her tears, turning resolutely toward the building. She was strong. He'd told her so.

But the sight of Tyler standing there made her stop short. Her heart seemed to jump into her throat and it took her a moment to form the words. "You didn't leave."

His eyes narrowed. "Didn't know I was supposed to."

"No." She turned and waved her hand at the departed helicopter. "When the helicopter left, I thought for sure you were on it."

"I wouldn't have left without saying goodbye, M." He held up a sheet of paper, and she recognized the fax that she'd left on the table in the office. "Congratulations. Looks like you're getting everything you wanted."

Her eyes burned. "Not everything," she managed.

Tyler's eyes sharpened. "Franco *is* headed back home?"

"Two soldiers are driving him back. They left quite a while ago." She pushed her hands in her pockets to keep from twisting them together. "Not that there was much of *la Fortuna* for him to go back to even if he'd wanted to."

"The sleeping quarters were left intact."

"I was told that." No matter what Franco had planned, Tyler had deliberately kept from taking innocent lives. "The communications center in the mansion was destroyed, though. El Jefe will have to scramble to regain even a portion of its control on the region." She tilted her head. "Obviously that pack of gum of yours had something to do with it all. But I don't see how something so small could do so much damage."

He was looking at the fax, folding it precisely in half. "I'm good at what I do. But it's not a very easy thing to accept *what* I do sometimes," he said.

Marisa pressed her lips together. "Sometimes necessary things aren't easy," she said. "Someone I know told me that." She had to force the words past her tight throat.

"And sometimes necessary things are as easy as breathing."

She didn't know what he meant by that. "Tyler, I'm sorry I kept the truth from you. If I had to do it over again, I—"

"God forbid."

Her lips pressed together. "Of course. Silly of me."

"Seeing you in danger, Marisa, I couldn't take it again."

Her breath stalled and hope congested her nerves. "What?"

He held the fax out to her. "Embassy service will suit you."

She took the paper and pushed it into her pocket. "Actually I've decided to turn it down." She'd come to that decision when she'd read the fax.

He looked stunned. "Why?"

"Because I'm done trying to please my parents by making a marriage they approve of, or taking a career that my mother can brag about. It's time for me to live my life on my terms. I love them, and I know they love me whether or not my mother can ever bring herself to admit it."

"What are you going to do?"

She swallowed. What had she accomplished in her life if not for taking chances? "I've been hearing about an interesting town in Texas," she said, taking a step closer to him. "Mission Creek, it's called. No rain forest in sight, which pleases me no end. I'm a good waitress. A good interpreter. I still have to finish that paper on the long-term effects of video game usage by myopic users. Though I'll have to get a new copy. My other one happened to be destroyed in a plane crash. Beyond that, I think I'll play it by ear."

"Is that your only requirement?"

She tilted her head back, looking into his face. He'd showered and cleaned up, just as she had, and looked unbearably handsome in his uniform. "It's where the man I love lives." She lifted a shoulder. "That's my only requirement."

He smiled a little, drew a loose curl away from her cheek, and her heart raced.

"What if he goes to Geneva in the fall?"

"French is spoken in Geneva. He may need an interpreter. *Parlez-vous français*?"

His smile widened. "I don't know, M. You're good at watching a guy's back, but traveling with you can get a little out of hand."

"Maybe I just need someone to show me how it's supposed to be, Murdoch."

He closed his hands over her face and gently lifted it. His eyes were serious. "I have a requirement of my own."

"What?"

"That you don't teach our kids Spanish before me. I love you, Marisa, but on this I've got to put my foot down."

She laughed, her tears escaping. She went onto her toes, kissing him, loving him. "It's going to take me fifty years to figure you out, Tyler Murdoch."

His hands swept down her back, holding her tight. "Then the first fifty are yours," he murmured in her ear. "But after that, it's my turn."

Epilogue

"Welcome back, Luke."

How many times had he heard just those words? Too damn many, Luke Callaghan figured. Someone had gotten a chair for him and as he sat there, he conjured a vision of the lobby of the Lone Star Country Club, where it seemed as if half the town had gathered.

Voices and laughter and music rose through the two-story lobby. Footsteps seemed loud against the pink granite tiles, and he even imagined he could hear the sound of the fountain over the commotion caused by the crowd.

It was his welcome home party, but Luke had never felt less like celebrating. He shoved at the sunglasses he wore. Unnecessary, as far as he was concerned, since he couldn't see one damn thing. Not one face, not one friend. Not one enemy.

His hands curled, frustration racing through him.

"Hold on to that," a voice said beside him. He felt the cool squat glass nudged against his hand, and he took it.

He recognized Tyler's voice. "I didn't think you were back from Central America, yet, buddy. Last I heard, you were still down there frolicking on the beach with some looker named Marisa."

He heard his friend laugh softly. "And miss this big do? Hell, Luke, you know me better 'n that."

"Yeah, a big damn party, while my baby girl is in the hands of God knows who."

Luke heard the scrape of a chair on the tile, and knew that Tyler had sat down beside him. He heard the soft clink of ice against glass. "I would've come back sooner if I'd heard about that. Lena's definitely yours, then?"

"The DNA test confirmed it."

"Is there anything new from the feds?"

His jaw ached. "No."

"And there's been no ransom demand?"

"No."

"Kind of odd, don't you think? Why else would someone kidnap Lena if not to milk you for some of your millions? The kidnapper must have known what we didn't until recently. That Lena was yours. So, why no ransom demand?"

If he knew that, he'd be one step closer to finding the daughter that he hadn't even known he'd had until recently. "Josie has a lot of pictures of her," he said roughly. "My daughter. And I can't see the damn things. I don't even know what Lena looks like.''

"She's beautiful," Tyler admitted. "And you'll be seeing her soon enough."

"It's gonna take a miracle, Ty." Luke wasn't sure he believed in miracles these days.

"I thought the docs said your blindness was temporary."

"Yeah, in a best-case scenario." Luke's voice dripped sarcasm. "They don't know anything for sure. Any more than we know for sure that Lena is ever going to be found. Or if she's even still—" He couldn't bring himself to say it.

Tyler clasped Luke's shoulder in a steady grip. "Miracles can happen, bud. If that's what it takes, then that's what you'll get."

A cloud of perfume assailed them, and Luke braced himself only moments before a feminine cheek pressed against his. "It's so good to have you home, Luke, honey."

He made himself smile, and was glad when the perfumed one moved off. "Who the hell was that?"

"Bitsy O'Malley."

"Who?"

"You dated her a few times last year."

"Oh." He dismissed the woman from his mind. He wasn't interested in *any* woman these days, except for the one who'd left their daughter in a carrier on a golf course nearly ten months ago. "And since when do *you* believe in miracles?"

"Since her," Tyler murmured.

Luke heard Tyler stand and he knew more people had neared them. He stood also, hating feeling like an invalid.

"Marisa, this is a friend of mine, Luke Callaghan. Luke, say hello to Marisa. My fiancée."

Luke absorbed that. He heard the note in Tyler's voice, a note he'd never had before. "Well, well. Fiancée, huh?" He felt a real smile tug at his lips, and unerringly lowered his head to kiss the woman's smooth cheek. "Now I know why Tyler's been babbling about miracles. Much happiness to you. But are you sure you know what you're taking on?"

"Absolutely," Marisa said in a pretty, slightly accented voice. "It's good to meet you, Luke. There's someone else here, too."

Luke found his hand clasped in a hard, firm grip. A grip he knew. "Colonel Westin."

"Good to see you up and around, son."

"You too, sir."

"I hear that you're having some trouble 'round here, again. You let me know if you need anything."

"Thank you, sir. I appreciate that."

"No, Luke. I appreciate what you've done for me. You and Tyler and the rest who didn't give up on me. Now, do me another favor."

"Anything, sir."

"Don't give up on finding your little girl. You boys are better at what you do than anyone else. If you don't like what the Bureau is saying, then work around them."

Luke slowly nodded. Westin was right. Blindness, temporary or not, didn't mean that he was incapable. He still had his brains. And he still had his friends. "I won't give up," he assured them all, suddenly feeling better than he had in weeks. "Not ever."

While the rafters of the Lone Star Country Club were being raised during Luke's welcome home celebration, rafters were being raised in nearby Goldenrod. Only there, it was from the impatient wail of a little lady with black hair and vivid blue eyes.

Erica Clawson shushed the baby. If Frank came by while the little mite was screaming her head off, he'd be angry with her. And Erica hated it when Frank got angry. She much preferred it when he was all lovin', and sweet-talking, and focusing entirely on her, instead of thinking about his old fiancée, Haley, or this baby.

She gave up trying to distract the baby with the stuffed toy and scooped her out of the crib, snuggling her close. She really was a sweet thing. Erica could almost feel bad for Daisy, who had to be going out of her mind knowing her kid had been snatched from the Carson Ranch.

But if Daisy really *was* Haley Mercado, back from the dead, then Erica's sympathies about dried up. She'd do anything for Frank. But she had no intentions of sharing him.

She pressed her lips to the baby's forehead and wandered out to the small kitchen. "Come on, Lena," she said gently. "How 'bout you and I have some peaches?"

* * * * *

Don't miss the next story from
Silhouette's

LONE STAR COUNTRY CLUB

THE LAST BACHELOR
by Judy Christenberry

Available February 2003

Turn the page for an excerpt from this
exciting romance…!

One

Joe Turner turned into the drive of the Lone Star Country Club. It was a little late for lunch, but that just meant the café wouldn't be packed. Maybe he'd have a little time to chat with Ginger.

He chuckled. He was a fool, of course. Ginger probably wasn't even twenty-one, and he was thirty-four. If he were precocious, he could claim to be old enough to be her father. But she always caught his eye.

And every other man's in the place.

It wasn't her curves that drew all the men's attention, though she certainly had some striking ones. It wasn't even her auburn hair and beautiful complexion. Or her big blue eyes. It was all of those things, actually, but it was her appearance of innocence that touched every man's heart. At least it did Joe's. Joe always had the belief that she was a princess in disguise who needed rescuing.

"Right!" he muttered, telling himself he was crazy.

The well-groomed driveway wound its way to the entrance of the country club. Joe was almost there when out of the corner of his eye he caught sight of a yellow apron the waitresses wore in the Yellow Rose Café. One of the employees was running from the parking lot toward the main highway.

Almost immediately he realized it was Ginger, her smooth hair blowing away from her face as she hurried. He knew she didn't have a car, but usually she caught a ride with one of the other girls. Besides, he knew her schedule. She worked until nine o'clock on Fridays.

He picked up speed and followed the circle up the other side, toward the highway. He pulled in front of Ginger and stopped, hurrying out of his car to intercept her.

"Ginger? Is something wrong?"

"Oh! Mr. Turner! No. Nothing is wrong."

"Then why are you crying?"

She self-consciously wiped her cheeks. "Uh, I— I don't feel well. I must go home." She started around him.

"Get in my car. I'll drive you home."

"No, I—" She looked back toward the country club. She abruptly changed her mind. "Okay!"

Joe looked behind Ginger and saw two men in dark suits getting into a dark car. It looked like a government car. With a frown, he slid behind the wheel again.

"Who are they?" he asked. He turned to look at

Ginger, only to discover she'd slid down in the seat, as if she were hiding. "Ginger, what's going on?"

"Please just take me home."

Her normally pale cheeks were flushed, and tears gathered in her light blue eyes. Joe could never refuse to help her. He put his Lexus in Drive and started toward the small apartment where Ginger lived. When he'd first realized Ginger lived in such a small place, he'd talked to Harvey Small, the manager of the club. He wanted Ginger to receive more pay so she could have a nicer apartment.

Joe drove slowly, studying Ginger out of the corner of his eye, trying to figure out what was wrong. She didn't give him many clues. She simply stared straight ahead, her teeth sunk into her bottom lip, and a frown on her face.

"Do you need me to take you to the doctor?"

"No! I need to go home."

"Okay," he agreed, trying to sound calm. But something was wrong.

They approached the small apartment house, and Joe figured he'd done his best for her. She obviously didn't want any help.

Suddenly she moaned. "No! No, no, no!"

He stopped at once. "Ginger, what's wrong? I'll help if you'll tell me."

"No one can help me now." Her mournful words broke his heart.

"Sweetheart, I promise I'll do what I can."

"Take me to—to the park, please." She had her eyes closed. Then she opened them and hurriedly said, "If you don't mind."

"Not at all." The park was across the street from the apartments. It was small with a few picnic tables and a basketball court that drew the neighborhood boys after school. Right now it appeared deserted.

He parked his Lexus in the empty parking lot. When he turned around, he saw Ginger staring into his rearview mirror. That was when he noticed the government car parked near Ginger's apartment.

"I think it's about time you explained to me what's going on. Obviously those two men are up-setting you. Shall I go talk to them?"

"No!" She seemed to pull herself together. "Mr. Turner, you've always been so nice, so generous. I know you want to help, but there's nothing to be done. If you don't know what's wrong, then you can't be accused of anything."

"Accused? Accused of what? There's nothing illegal about giving a ride to a friend."

Ginger Walton looked at the man beside her with gratitude. He'd called her a friend. He'd come back to his hometown a few months ago to supervise the rebuilding on the country club. There had been a bombing of it that had destroyed the prestigious Men's Grill. Joe Turner was an architect from Chicago, but he'd moved back to Mission Creek to do the work.

He'd been friendly the first time she'd served him. Ginger had loved waiting on him because he treated her with respect. He didn't try to get familiar with her or ask her out. Now he called her his friend.

But she couldn't get him in trouble. With a sigh, she suggested he go back to the country club for lunch.

"So what are you going to do?" he asked.

She didn't have an answer for him. As long as those men were there, waiting for her, she couldn't go home. And she couldn't leave until she got her money out of there. She should've put it in a bank. But she'd cashed her paychecks and hidden in her apartment the money she didn't need to pay bills. So she could leave quickly when she had to.

"Ginger?"

It took her a moment to remember his question. "Uh, I don't know."

"Are those men looking for you?"

"They are looking for Virvela Waltek," she admitted with a sob.

Joe frowned at her. "Who's that?"

She sniffed. It was so very hard to admit the truth. Finally she whispered, "Me."

LONE STAR LSCC COUNTRY CLUB EST. 1923

If you missed the first exciting stories from the Lone Star Country Club, here's a chance to order your copies today!

0-373-61352-0	STROKE OF FORTUNE by Christine Rimmer	___ $4.75 U.S.	___ $5.75 CAN.
0-373-61353-9	TEXAS ROSE by Marie Ferrarella	___ $4.75 U.S.	___ $5.75 CAN.
0-373-61354-7	THE REBEL'S RETURN by Beverly Barton	___ $4.75 U.S.	___ $5.75 CAN.
0-373-61355-5	HEARTBREAKER by Laurie Paige	___ $4.75 U.S.	___ $5.75 CAN.
0-373-61356-3	PROMISED TO A SHEIK by Carla Cassidy	___ $4.75 U.S.	___ $5.75 CAN.
0-373-61357-1	THE QUIET SEDUCTION by Dixie Browning	___ $4.75 U.S.	___ $5.75 CAN.
0-373-61358-X	AN ARRANGED MARRIAGE by Peggy Moreland	___ $4.75 U.S.	___ $5.75 CAN.

(Limited quantities available.)

TOTAL AMOUNT	$_____
POSTAGE & HANDLING	$_____
($1.00 for one book, 50¢ for each additional)	
APPLICABLE TAXES*	$_____
TOTAL PAYABLE	$_____

(Check or money order—please do not send cash)

To order, send the completed form along with your name, address, zip or postal code, along with a check or money order for the total above, payable to **Lone Star Country Club,** to:

In the U.S.: 3010 Walden Avenue, P.O. Box 9047, Buffalo, NY 14269-9047; **In Canada:** P.O. Box 616, Fort Erie, Ontario L2A 5X3

Name:_____

Address:_____ City:_____

State/Prov:_____ Zip/Postal Code:_____

Account Number (if applicable):_____

093 KJH DNC 3

*New York residents remit applicable sales taxes.
*Canadian residents remit applicable GST and provincial taxes.

Visit us at www.lonestarcountryclub.com   LSCCBACK-7